Fiddler
in the
Boardroom

A Trilogy of Financial Scandals

Francis A. Andrew

Order this book online at www.trafford.com
or email orders@trafford.com

Most Trafford titles are also available at major online book retailers.

Printed in the United States of America.

ISBN: 978-1-4269-3731-6 (sc)
ISBN: 978-1-4269-3732-3 (e)

Library of Congress Control Number: 2010910310

Trafford rev. 02/09/2012

 www.trafford.com

North America & international
toll-free: 1 888 232 4444 (USA & Canada)
phone: 250 383 6864 ♦ fax: 812 355 4082

Space Tours, Inc.

I.

Scarrowgate in Yorkshire is an average sized town which boasts an average sized lunatic asylum. Though its official title is *A Home of Relaxation for the Mentally Ill-At-Ease* it is more often than not referred to by the less politically correct locals as the "nut'ouse", or "the loony bin", "funny farm", or just simply "the nutter".

Whatever connotation we may ascribe to the "mentally ill-at-ease" who shelter behind the Home's protective walls, there is one common thread which links the inmates and which tends to confer a tempering effect upon those of either charitable or uncharitable disposition who respectively refer to the residents as "mentally disturbed" and "nuts" - and that is – private mental medicine: you definitely can't be short of a bob or two to get your napper examined here!

By the year 2030, advances in space technology have made it possible for those of more moderate means to travel beyond the confines of the Earth and out into the solar system. Instead of paying millions, about a hundred thousand pounds sterling will get you as far as the Oort Cloud and back.

Space Tours, Inc. have refined the technology just that tad more to bring the price down to a mere fifty thousand pounds. Not only that, but for your fifty grand you get restaurant and bar facilities, gymnasium and health club with sauna and jacuzzi, a luxury bedroom with 24 hour room service and a beautiful blonde to rub you down in the massage parlour.

Dr. Casper Brians, the governor of the Scarrowgate lunatic asylum had a visit from no less a personage than Mr. Bernie Rocks, the Chairman of the Board of *Space Tours, Inc.* Mr. Rocks was a small dumpy man in his middle fifties. He did not claim to be an astronaut of any description, he just "devised policy and kept the company accounts on an even keel". Mr. Rocks was accompanied by the Deputy Chairman, Mr. Reggie Guggins, the Marketing Director, Mr. Pete Proster, and the Advertising Director, Mrs. Judith Chambers.

"You say Mr. Rocks that your organisation not only caters for the adventurous space tourist but can actually be a restorative for the mentally ill", said Dr. Brians.

"Indeed, that is so, Dr. Brians", replied Rocks in a tone of solemnity.

"I am a trained psychiatrist, Mr. Rocks, and I fail to see how that can be so. With respect to both you and your Board members, you are not trained in this discipline."

"Well, we've consulted other psychiatrists who testify to the therapeutic properties of space travel", said Pete Proster.

"Who exactly are they?", asked Dr. Brians.

"I can't exactly remember their names off-hand".

"Well, I would have thought that you would have come here with not only their names but with written attestations so necessary to back up such a controversial claim".

"Other space tour organizations such as the Australian company *Solar System Rides* have claimed great successes for mentally ill patients who embarked upon journeys with them", said Mrs. Judith Chambers in her somewhat abrupt schoolmarmish tone of voice.

"You may check that on the internet, Dr. Brians", Bernie Rocks advised the asylum governor.

"Mrs. Chambers, gentlemen, in our profession, we require more than looking at websites. We need proven track records attested by qualified psychiatrists and subject to peer review after publication in professional psychiatric journals."

"Will you at least consider it, Dr. Brians?" Reggie Guggins asked.

"I have considered it, and the answer is no. I cannot possibly allow patients suffering from severe mental trauma to undergo a very risky journey through the solar system."

"There is absolutely no risk at all, Dr. Brians", the Chairman of *Space Tours Inc.* advised the asylum governor. "In fact", he went on, "I can give a 100% guarantee that no harm shall befall them on their journey to the planets."

The other Board members looked at the Chairman, who looked at them, who all looked at Dr. Brians, who looked back at them and then to the Chairman. And accompanying all this looking were the heads of the Board members bobbing up and down in nodding agreement.

"Mr. Rocks!" said Brians in a highly indignant tone, "how can you possibly utter such assurances and offer such guarantees with such absolute and utter certainty? May I dare say it – but this is complete madness? I'm now beginning to wonder where the true lunacy lies, here in this asylum, or in the boardroom at *Space Tours Inc.* Now madam, gentlemen", continued Dr. Brians who was now rising from his chair and going crimson red in the fact, "we have taken up enough of each others' time. I bid you all good day."

Dr. Brians walked over to his office door and held it open for his guests. Guggins, Prostor and Chambers dejectedly trundled out. Rocks however remained behind.

"Mr. Rocks, I think I made myself quite clear regarding bringing this matter to a close", said Brians somewhat pompously.

"Dr. Brians, I beg of you, please give me just a few more minutes of your precious time and I will explain the reason for giving such assurances of safety with such confidence."

"Very well, but a few minutes only. Five to be precise and starting two minutes ago."

II.

The two hundred inmates of the Scarrowgate *Home of Relaxation for the Mentally Ill-At- Ease* were assembled in that grand edifice's main hall. Taking their places on the podium were Dr. Casper Brians, the governor of the *Home*, Mr. Bernie Rocks and his three senior Board members, and Captain Trevor Blump and First Officer Sammy Slyme.

Dr. Brians began to address the audience of patients, doctors and nursing staff. "Ladies and gentlemen. It gives me great pleasure to introduce to you Mr. Bernie Rocks the Chairman and Chief Executive of *Space Tours, Inc.*"

Oh how old Rocks loved the "chief executive" bit being thrown in by Brians. It was the sort of ego stroking in which Rocks just wallowed with delight. Brians went on to introduce the other members of the Board. As he had done in his introduction of Rocks, the ego-stroking exercise continued with the others being afforded those extra tid bits appended to their boardroom titles.

"Now", continued the asylum governor, "I am sure you have all heard of the various space travel organisations which can, due to great advances in technology, take passengers into deep space, in fact, right to the edge of the solar system. But technology has advanced that one step further in Mr. Rocks' *Space Tours, Inc.*. Thanks to developments in production, assembly, fuel research and much much more, *Space Tours, Inc.* can now offer solar system tours at half the normal cost of its competitors. For a mere 50,000 pounds, you can have the most spectacular cruise of the solar system. Yet, ladies and gentlemen, it gets even better. Mr. Rocks and his Board have decided to provide a special rate for guests of this *Home.* You can have this three month cruise of a lifetime for only 40,000 pounds. And there's more. The spaceship is a flying deluxe hotel. It will be just as if you had booked into the likes of the Hilton, Claridges or the Four Seasons; the only difference being, you will be flying through the solar system.

"Now you may be wondering as to what all this has to do with your various conditions and disorders. Well, recent psychiatric research, backed up by evidence and peer review, has shown the amazing therapeutic wonders of space travel. When patients have gone up into space and seen the Earth from hundreds of miles above its surface and then gone further on to see the magnificent variety of stunning sights of other worlds, they forget all their problems. In fact, they forget that they are even mentally sick. Once they have returned to Earth, they are completely cured of their ailments.

"I want you to consider this proposition carefully before you make a decision. In the meantime, are there any questions you might like to ask?"

"What about safety?" one of the nurses asked.

"Captain Blump, you would be the most qualified person here to answer that question."

"Our ship is designed to incorporate a large number of safety features. Furthermore, we have smaller 'lifeboat' vessels on board incase of total breakdown of the mother ship." At this point Blump invited the craft's Chief Engineer, Rupert Tremis to elaborate on the issue.

"When I sent the plan of the new ship and all its safety features to the University of Oxford, their mathematicians calculated that the odds of any serious mishap are 1 in 20 million. Now you can't get much safer than that", explained Rupert Tremis.

"You say you can get around the solar system in only three months", asked one of the doctors. "How do you achieve such humongous speeds?"

The ship's navigator, Roddy Watts took the question. "We have developed a kind of propulsion system that uses nuclear fuel far more efficiently than older types of spacecraft do. Our metallurgists have developed such tensile material that the high speeds involved will not damage the craft".

"Has that theory been put to the test?" asked Vincent MacGregor, an inmate suffering from severe manic depression.

"Yes it has", said the ship's First Officer, Sammy Slyme. "Last year, we sent the ship on a remote controlled tour through the solar system. When it landed on Earth, there wasn't even a scratch on it".

After some more questions, answers and explanations, Dr. Brians declared the meeting closed. "Go back to your rooms and think about this over the next few days. If you feel it is for you, come and see me in my office where we can make the arrangements for your trip".

III.

Three days after the space tour hype, Dr. Brians was seated at his office desk. The governor of the asylum was shuffling through some papers, and hovering above Brians with somewhat of a studious countenance was none other than Bernie Rocks examining those same papers.

"So far we have only four signed up for the trip, Mr. Rocks", said the governor in rather subdued tones.

"Any chance of persuading a few more to come on board?" Rocks asked in tones hopeful of a reply in the affirmative.

Without even glancing upwards at Rocks, Brians simply shook his head. "You know Rocks, once more people come to know about the wonders of your tours and the safety involved, you'll probably get more signing up".

Rocks did not reply to this. He simply took out a small pocket calculator and starting pressing away at the buttons. "At best we break even on only four, at worst, we make a slight loss", he said after ten minutes of some arithmetic.

"Although I'm a psychiatrist by training, I have had some experience in business. This asylum is in the private sector and receives no government grants or funding from NGOs. So - may I suggest something, Rocks?"

"Go ahead" was all that Rocks said in reply. "But whatever you have to say Brians, business is business and we can't run a business at a loss".

"All right; here is my suggestion: take a slight loss. Put the loss involved in this trip down to advertising expenses. You'll more than make up for it in subsequent trips".

"Can you be sure that this will work?" asked the Chairman of *Space Tours, Inc.* "That is the theory, what about this idea working in practice?"

"We ran at a slight loss with this asylum for a year, at break even for six months, then at a small profit for another six months. As our successes in the new psychiatric techniques became more widely known, our profits have continued to go onwards and upwards."

"All right", sighed Rocks as he picked up his leather briefcase and made his way towards the door, "I'll put this idea to my fellow Board members and then get back to you on our decision".

A few days later, Brians' telephone rang. Bernie Rocks was on the other end. He informed Brians that the Board had unanimously agreed to go ahead with the pilot programme and that he, Rocks, would be coming over to the asylum to see the passengers.

"So when exactly do you plan to start the tour, Mr. Rocks?" Brians asked the Chairman when the latter had come to call on him later that morning.

"First of all, when we have the money; and then when your inmates are packed and ready", replied Rocks.

"I gave them your bank details two days ago. If you check your account, I think you will find that 160,000 pounds has been deposited in it."

Rocks took out his miniature laptop. He accessed his company's bank account and found to his great satisfaction that the afore-mentioned sum had indeed been deposited there. Next, he contacted Captain Trevor Blump and asked him when it would be possible to launch into outer space. After a few minutes of conversation with the captain of the space vessel, Rocks asked Brians to inform the four inmates that blast off was to be seven days hence. Next, Rocks wanted to know about the inmates who would soon be the space tourists.

"It would be an excellent idea for the crew of your spacecraft to meet the four passengers prior to take-off", Dr. Brians advised. "A sort of 'getting to know you', type thing, if you see what I mean".

"Could they come tomorrow and see around the ship and meet the crew members?"

"I see no reason as to why not. Now where exactly is your ship located? I mean where is the launching pad?"

"It's in a converted five acre field. It's sheltered in a massive hangar where our mechanics and technicians are getting it ready for its flight. Dr. Brians, we'll send one of our company's mini-buses to take you and your four patients to see around the craft. Shall we say tomorrow morning at 10 o'clock?"

"That I am sure will be all right. Of course if there is any problem with that, I'll let you know and we can make some alternative arrangements. However, in the meantime, if you don't hear from me, just assume that the 10am arrangement is unaltered".

"Fine", said Rocks "just fine. Now, would it be possible for you, Dr. Brians to give me some briefing on the four patients who have opted to go on the tour?"

"Yes", began Brians in sombre tones. "First of all let me begin with Mr. Alfred Sharples. He is a publican. Over the years he has built up a chain of pubs throughout Britain. You've no doubt heard of the *Sharples Houses of Refreshment*?

"Oh yes", replied Rocks. "I often had a drink or six at his establishments! And, what brings him here - I mean someone who appears to have everything in life going for him?"

"Well, often he has been his own best customer at the bar. He has been diagnosed as an alcoholic."

"But what is at the basis of his drinking? Surely there is something more psychologically deep-rooted and the drinking is just a symptom of it".

"About 20 years ago, he was madly in love. But she rejected his proposal of marriage. So he tried to prove his worthiness of the young lady. To do that he scrimped and saved all his earnings and set up first one pub, then another, and, to cut a long story short, a whole chain of them were established within five years. However, the lady in question was still not interested in him despite his multimillionaire status. It was too much for him – hence the heavy drinking."

"How does he manage to run his eh houses of refreshment when he's here?" wondered Rocks.

"Oh, that has an in-built management structure. He's got people there to take care of everything. In fact, one part of the duties of the staff was to carry out a blind drunk Mr. Sharples from the pub every night and bundle him into his awaiting chauffeur driven Rolls Royce".

"So, who do we have next?" asked Rocks.

"The next name is Miss Susan Blyth. She is a manic depressive. She's a businesswoman of some description".

"What kind of business?"

"I don't know. It's a largish family concern. Oh they have their fingers in quite a few pies. Then we have a certain Vincent MacGregor. Scottish as you can well imagine."

"And what's his background?"

"He's a bit of a mystery man. He suffers from depression but we don't know why. We don't really know much about his family or occupational background but he doesn't seem to be short on the filthy lucre. I reckon it's inherited – old money".

"Right then – who's our fourth passenger?"

"Mrs. Elizabeth Walters. She suffers from a kind of schizophrenia. She imagines herself to be all sorts of things. Catherine the Great one day, Josephine Bonaparte the next."

"So is everyone ready? We have the bus waiting outside. Are you coming with us Dr. Brians? I mean – just to look around."

"Yes indeed – why not. Of course, I'm just far too busy to come on the trip."

Rocks and Brians went downstairs to the front of the asylum where the four passengers were waiting for orders to board the bus. After the four patients were personally introduced to Mr. Rocks, everyone climbed onto the bus. Thirty minutes later, the bus paused at a massively large hangar in a field miles from no-where.

Everyone alighted from the bus and were guided over to the massive doors of the massive hangar by a couple of

Rocks' security guards. The doors slid open and the party went inside.

The awe-struck patients and Dr. Brians saw before them a gigantic octagonal structure which stood about100 feet high and about 3000 feet in diameter. It looked something like a cross between a futuristic building and a flying saucer. There were eight powerful looking engines attached to the structure – one at each end of the octagon.

"Come this way, ladies and gentlemen", said Rocks to his visitors. Rocks led the way to a panel on the craft. He took a small devise like object from his pocket and pressed a few buttons on it. The panel parted in two and Rocks led the way inside the mysterious craft.

"Welcome to your ship" continued Rocks. "She has been christened *The Interplanetary Voyager*. She will be your home for the next three months as you make your exciting journey throughout the solar system. This part of the ship you are now in is the airlock. Exit and entry is by this means." Rocks pressed a button on one of the walls and another panel section slid open. This led them into the foyer of the flying hotel. It was sheer luxury – exotic plants and studded leather chairs were strewn around the vast open area.

The next hour was spent on a tour around the spacecraft. The guests saw the Olympic sized pool, the gymnasium, the sports area, two bars and five restaurants – Italian, Chinese, Greek, French and Turkish.

They were then shown their rooms which had all the creature comforts one could imagine. Each room was equipped with a fifteen foot square viewer. This would enable them to see into outer space in the direction of the ship's travel. "I would suggest", said Rocks, "that if you want to see the moon and the planets in all their glory and brilliance, go to the cinema. When we are near a planet we shall relay the pictures to the large 50 foot screen from our cameras which are attached to the outside of the spaceship. I assure you, the views are breathtaking."

At the end of the tour, the four guests were introduced to the four senior members of the crew – Captain Trevor Blump, First Officer Sam Slyme, Engineer Rupert Tremis and Navigator Roddy Watts. They showed them around the control room which looked highly sophisticated with its array of the latest computers, navigation and steering equipment and 40 foot square viewing monitor. Outside of the control rooms and down in the foyer, the restaurant, bar and room service staff were lined up military fashion to greet the four VIPs.

At the end of the tour around the craft, Rocks bid his guests farewell. On behalf of all the crew members, Captain Blump said he looked forward to seeing his most esteemed guests the following week when they would be embarking upon the adventure of a lifetime.

IV.

The following week, Captain Blump and First Officer Sam Slyme were there to greet the four guests who, with packed suitcases, trundled through the air-lock and into the hotel-like foyer of the craft.

"Are there any questions you would like to ask?" said Blump to the four passengers.

"Yes", answered MacGregor. "Should we not be well strapped into our seats ready for take-off as the acceleration will have a highly stressful effect on our bodies?"

"Not on this craft, Mr. MacGregor", replied Blump. "We have specially designed this craft to eliminate the effects on the human body during take-off. In fact you can have a drink at the bar and watch the video monitor where you will view our ascent."

"What about weightlessness while we are in space?" asked Susan Blyth.

"Oh that's been well taken care of as well", said Slyme. "Underneath the ship there is a structure containing super-magnets. The rotation of this structure along with the effects of the super-magnets creates artificial gravity. So don't worry – you won't be floating about like clouds during your holiday."

"How do we blast off from inside the hangar?" Elizabeth Walters asked.

"Easy", replied Roddy Watts, "the roof of the hanger opens and the ship just glides upwards".

The four guests decided to make for the cinema to watch the take-off on the large screen. Upwards and upwards went the craft and ever onwards went the "ooos" and "aaaahs" as the Earth beneath them became smaller and smaller. And the "ooos" and the "aaaahs" started up again a day later as the passengers and crew watched the moon grow larger and larger on their monitor screens. When it came to viewing the moon close up, the passengers went to the large viewing screen in the cinema.

"We are now in orbit around the moon", Roddy Watts, the chief navigator told his guests when they were assembled in the cinema's auditorium. "Isn't that a wonderful sight to behold? And just wait until the craft passes round to the dark side of the moon. You'll be awestruck. It's the side of the moon that never faces the Earth".

"I just wonder", queried Alfred Sharples, "if there is any chance that this craft could land on the moon and that we could take a walk around the lunar surface".

"Well, now that is a design feature that this craft is lacking", responded Watts. "We cannot land on an astronomical body with low gravity, or for that matter one with too much gravity. Our engineers are working on this problem and we hope that within a year or two we will be offering lunar package holidays. In the meantime, our crafts can only take off from and land on the Earth."

One month went by and the passengers were treated to the most amazing panoramic sights of the three inner planets. No shortage of the "ooos" and "aaaahs" as the four guests sat with fixated gazes on the monitoring screen in the craft's cinema.

"I thought that our approaches to Venus and Mercury would have resulted in an increase in temperature", Elizabeth Walters asked Sam Slyme in the Italian restaurant one day."

"Oh", answered Slyme in rather dismissive tones, "that's so easy to cope with. This craft has an automatic temperature adjustment mechanism to deal with the extremes of conditions throughout the solar system".

And so the weeks and months rolled on and the four worthy guests were completely bowled over by the spectacular views of the giant planet Jupiter and the ringed planet Saturn. Onwards they went past Uranus, Neptune and Pluto. They saw the billions of comets in the Oort Cloud which encircle the solar system like a halo.

And so the return journey to Earth began. All throughout the journey passengers and crew stuck to the 24 hour Earth day. Although this had no astronomical relevance outside of the Earth's rotational period, internal body clocks remained unaltered. So, one "evening" the four passengers were invited by the senior members of the crew to a special dinner in the Italian restaurant. Blump, Slyme, Watts and Tremis wanted to investigate the effects of the trip on the passengers.

"Frankly, I don't feel that it has done anything to help me with my drink problem", Alfred Sharples told Blump and his fellow crew members.

"Well, I think it has done me wonders", said Elizabeth Walters in contradiction to Sharples' negative assessment.

"I must say I'm glad to hear that", said Slyme.

"When I get back to Earth", continued Mrs. Walters, "I'm going to tell my husband, the Emperor Napoleon all about it."

"Ah yes, I see, I see", said Blump with much disappointment in his tone.

"What about you Miss Blyth?" Rupert Tremis asked Susan Blyth the manic depressive.

"I really don't know. I can't really say", replied Susan as she slowly chewed on a chicken drumstick.

"Why is that?" continued Trevis.

"Because I feel so depressed", was Susan's reply.

"What about you Mr. MacGregor? Has this trip had a positive impact upon you?"

"Indeed Mr. Trevis, it has. It most truly has. I have learned such a lot. So much has been revealed to me that I cannot say how delighted I am. When this journey is over, when we are back on Earth again, there is so much that I am going to talk and write about."

At this joyous outburst from MacGregor, Blump's and his crew's countenances lit up. It was just what they needed – at least one passenger made a positive statement; they counted their blessings that there was at least one satisfied customer.

"There's still time yet for this trip to be the pick-me-up that it was hoped to be for you all", Blump said reassuringly to the three yet to be convinced passengers. "We'll be making our way back home again and we'll have a second chance to see the planets one more time. Now isn't that something to look forward to?"

Sharples, Blyth and Walters gave rather unconvincing nods. Only MacGregor was a bit more positive.

"By the way, Captain", said MacGregor addressing Blump, "speaking of pick-me-ups, I think Mr. Sharples needs one right now – quite literally."

Everyone looked around for their friend, but Alfred was no-where to be seen. Crew and passengers started to have puzzled looks on their faces. Eventually there was a little shuffling underneath the table. Gazing downwards, everyone saw Mr. Sharples. He was totally out for the count. Blump summoned over a waiter and whispered something in his ear. The waiter left and returned with another waiter. Both waiters helped poor old Alfred to his feet and escorted him to his bedroom.

"He'll be all right in the morning", said MacGregor. "This is a regular occurrence with him".

The meal was finished in silence and everyone slowly rose from the table and went off to their rooms.

V.

At around 2am, Earth time, Alfred Sharples woke up with a splitting headache. He was in a state of severe depression. He went for his whisky bottle and poured himself out a glassful. Slowly, he started sipping. When he had finished that, he took another, and then another, and yet another.

"If even a trip around the bloody solar system doesn't get my mind off Jennifer Low, then nothing will. What am I supposed to do? Take a trip around the God-damn galaxy?"

Alfred continued his reasoning with himself as he poured himself another drink. A few more drinks later and his reasoning powers became completely impaired.

"Sod this for a lark! Life isn't worth living. I'm going to end it all. Oh I know I've said this so many times before but I've never seemed to be able to pluck up the bleedin' courage to do it. Anyway I'm determined this time."

Alfred rose from his chair, staggered a bit and then managed to steady himself. He clutched the whisky bottle in his right hand and took a long slug from it. Then he opened his bedroom door and made his way down to the foyer of the craft. Once there he walked over to the airlock.

For a few days now, Alfred had been contemplating this move. He now felt he had the guts to do the awful deed. It would be quick, it would be painless – and it would be dramatic. The airless void in space combined with the deadly cosmic rays would finish him off in a split second. He took another mouthful from the bottle – ah just that last swig before stepping into the black void of space. Maybe some alien would find his body and revive him with highly advanced technology. But Alfred didn't care. He pressed the button on the airlock, the doors parted and Alfred stepped inside.

Before he pressed the button to open the doors which would take him into the eternity of the cosmos, Alfred drained off the remains of his whisky bottle. At first he hesitated before the button. He raised his hand towards it. Again he hesitated. He repeated this procedure three or four times. Eventually, Alfred pressed the button, the doors opened and Alfred stepped out into the darkness.

Vincent MacGregor left his room at around 2.45am. He walked soberly and straight. He went down to the foyer and over to the airlock. Without any hesitation, he pressed the button of the doors to the airlock. Anyone observing the contrast in the ways between Alfred's and Vincent's approaches to suicide would have been convinced of the sheer bravery of the latter of these two gentlemen. Then, once inside the airlock, without any hesitation or ceremony Vincent pressed the button. With total ease he stepped out of the parted doors and – into the dark voids of the cosmos? In fact, he stepped onto terra firma. There in front of him was Alfred Sharples lying dead drunk in a pool of vomit, his empty whisky bottle nearby.

"Good God – what the hell is this?" exclaimed MacGregor as he ran towards and crouched down beside the drunk man. He tapped Alfred on the shoulders. After a minute or two, he started to come round. Slowly he pushed himself up into a couched kneeling position.

"Are you God or maybe the Devil? Is this Hell? Where am I? Somebody, somebody …". Alfred then vomited violently.

Vincent backed away saying, "don't puke on me".

"What place is this? What world have I landed on?"

"It's the Earth. And you haven't landed on it. In fact you've never been off the damned place."

Alfred looked around himself. He recognised the massive hangar and the massive 'spaceship cum hotel'. "But… but…. how? I….I I don't get it".

"Come on back into the hotel and I'll explain it all to you. Quickly before Blump and the others are alerted."

MacGregor escorted Sharples back to his room. Sharples sat himself down in the big easy chair.

"So what the blazes is all this about?" Sharples asked. The shock of what he had seen had had an unexpected sobering effect on him.

"First of all", replied MacGregor, "go and take a shower and clean that puke off of yourself".

When Sharples had showered, he staggered through into the main room where MacGregor had made a large mug of strong black coffee for him.

"Here, drink this!" commanded MacGregor. Sharples clutched the cup and began drinking its contents thirstily. "And another thing", continued MacGregor, "that's the strongest you're going to drink for the rest of this …eh trip. That is if you want my co-operation in sorting out these con artists".

"How can you? How did you know about this?" asked the bleary eyed Alfred Sharples.

"I've been coming out here every night since we, since we eh – took off so to speak. I knew this was a con right from the start."

"How were you the only one not fooled by this charade? And why have you been leaving this hotel, craft or whatever the hell it is?"

"Okay, okay man. One question at a time. How do I know all this?! I'm Dr. Vincent MacGregor, professor of physics at St. Andrew's University. The explanations given by Blump and companions about such things as artificial gravity, no affects on the body during take-off and the ability of this craft to land and take off only on the Earth is balderdash."

"But artificial gravity has been achieved. Weren't the techniques for that worked out about five years ago?"

"Yes, but not according to the hair-brained explanation given by this lot".

"So, their scientific explanations don't make any sense?"

"No of course not, they're talking a pile of shite. Now regarding your other question as to what I am doing every night – I'd rather just keep mum on that for the moment."

"So what em er eh, why em are you at the home…. em?"

"You mean why am I at the nut-house? Well, I suffer occasional bouts of depression."

"I take it than Blump and co. don't know that you're a scientist".

"Of course not; they'd have found some excuse for preventing me from going."

"But wouldn't Dr. Brians have told them?"

"He doesn't know either. He thinks I'm a car dealer. It would look bad if faculty and students at St. Andy's knew I were taking courses of therapy at the nutter from time to time."

"Do you think Casper Brians is in on this?"

"Most definitely."

"How can you be sure about that?"

"I know", said MacGregor firmly. "All will be revealed in good time".

"What about the waiters, barmen, cleaning staff, room service and all the rest? How can so many people keep all this a secret. Surely someone, sometime, somewhere is going to let the cat out of the bag".

"Oh I doubt if anyone beyond Blump, Slyme, Tremis and Watts know about this. The hotel staff are as much conned as the passengers. Ha ha – and as for *chief* engineer and *chief* navigator and *first* officer – it's bullshit, there are no more 'crew' than Blump and his three cohorts".

"One more question: why didn't you just walk out of this joint long ago and call the police? You could have blown the whistle on this lot ages ago".

"First of all, it's not that easy. This hangar is surrounded by the company's armed guards."

"And second of all?"

"It's part of my plan not to say anything right now, even if I could. Trust me – I'm up to something that will be of great benefit to you, me and the other two passengers."

"What is that? How?"

"Just be patient. As I said – trust me and all in good time. Now Mr. Alfred Sharples, for the next six weeks, you're not going to touch anything stronger than coffee. Keep off the booze – not another drop. I don't want you to get blazing bloody drunk and spilling the beans on this."

"Here", replied Sharples handing over a whisky bottle to MacGregor, "take this. It's all I've got left. I promise you I won't touch another drop."

"I'll be keeping a sharp eye on you, Mr. Sharples".

VI.

"I was just wondering", said MacGregor to Blump over breakfast one morning", would it be at all possible to land the ship somewhere in Australia.? I'd like to get off there and visit some relatives. I'll eventually make my own way back to the UK."

"Well, eh", replied Blump rather hesitatingly, "it's the eh law you see. Patients must be returned back to the hospital or asylum."

"That law only applies to government run clinics", said Susan Blyth. "It doesn't cover the private sector".

"So then", intervened Elizabeth Walters, "you can drop Mr. MacGregor off in Australia and let me off in France".

"Ms Walters?" said Sam Slyme, "why on earth would you want to be let off in France?"

"Well to see my husband, the Emperor Napoleon Bonaparte of course".

"So there you are, said Alfred Sharples to Blump and Guggins. We could all be dropped off at different places and you're perfectly within the law".

By this time Blump was at a loss for words. However, his chief navigator came to the rescue. Roddy Watts told the passengers that the ship was pre-programmed to land in its exact spot in the hangar. A ship of such a size could not take off and land so many times. It was far too bulky for that. Blyth and Walters, along with their bacon and egg, swallowed all of this whole.

The crew and passengers went silent for a few minutes as they ate their breakfast. Susan Blyth was observed by the others to be reading a label on a packet of cream crackers. She had a somewhat puzzled look on her face. She was the first to break the silence. "Captain?" she said in a querying tone. And without raising her head from the packet of cream crackers continued, "emm eh – how comes it that the date on this packet of crackers is July 16th and we took off on June 28th?"

Blump went completely pale. He realised what a gaff he had made. He obviously had to do some pretty quick thinking here. "You see Ms Blyth, em, well, the company always post dates the products it delivers to us. Just incase we enter a time warp or something eh eh we want the produce to remain fresh. So if uhh we were transported into the future, our food would still be fresh".

"Old Blumpie was really scraping the bottom of the barrel there", Sharples said to MacGregor as they were leaving the dining room.

"Good old Susan", she really had him stumped on that one", replied MacGregor.

The six weeks passed by uneventfully and eventually it was time to end the imaginary journey through the solar system. Alfred Sharples managed to keep off the bottle and nothing of the fact that he and MacGregor knew of the fraud was made known to the crew and staff of the fantasy spaceship.

Vincent MacGregor continued his mysterious work outside the strange windowless hotel at night but he never told Sharples exactly what he was up to. However, on the night before the day that the spaceship was supposed to be landing on Earth, MacGregor asked Sharples to accompany him outside the craft.

"So are you going to tell me what you've been doing outside of here these past three months?" Sharples asked.

"Not exactly yet. I'd rather keep all that as a sort of grand finale – for you and the rest of the passengers and crew." MacGregor then took a miniature DVD camera from his pocket. He climbed up a ladder which took him to the deck where the cameras that were producing the space images were located. He plugged it into the main camera and looked into the viewing monitor for a minute or two. Then, he unplugged the device and came down to where Sharples was standing waiting for him.

"Now", said MacGregor producing a couple of whisky bottles, "take this one and I'll keep hold of the other". Sharples did as his friend asked him. MacGregor then walked about 15 feet from where they were standing and looked into the camera's viewer. He pressed a button on the device; there was then a slight buzzing sound and MacGregor let go of the camera. To Sharples' astonishment, the camera hovered stationery in the air. MacGregor then walked back to Sharples.

"Sit down please Alfred". Sharples obediently did so and MacGregor sat down about three feet away from him. Both men were still clutching their whisky bottles. MacGregor then told him exactly what to do.

Two minutes later, MacGregor walked over to his miniature camera and switched off the hovering mechanism on it. He then took the camera and once again ascended to where the spacecraft's cameras were located. One more time he plugged his camera into the craft's main camera and performed a few intricate operations. Finally, he unplugged his miniature camera, tucked it away in his shoulder bag and descended from the deck.

"What the blazes was that all about?" Sharples asked.

"You'll see soon enough".

The following morning the crew, passengers and all the staff were assembled in the cinema. They wanted to see the landing on the big screen.

"Well, now ladies and gentlemen", said Captain Blump, "in about half an hour we will be in orbit around the Earth. I hope you have all enjoyed your trip around the solar system. It will, I am sure, be the envy of all your family and friends. And also, I hope that you have medically benefited from your long three month journey. I trust that you will be able to leave the asylum and return to normal life." The captain went on in this mode for a full five minutes.

"When do we blow the whistle and expose this whole bloody charade?" Sharples asked MacGregor.

"Don't say one damned word until I tell you", said MacGregor in reply. "If you say anything prematurely, it will ruin everything I've been planning for the last three months."

Everyone now watched the large screen. But instead of seeing the large blue marble of the Earth that they had been expecting, their breath was taken away by utter shock when up on the massive viewing monitor was the ringed planet Saturn. And what caused them to almost have kittens was when they saw Alfred Sharples and Vincent MacGregor sitting on the rings of the massive planet, swigging away from bottles of whisky like a pair of drunks.

"So that's what you've been up to", Sharples whispered to MacGregor. "So this now is the grand finale".

"Grand Finale", MacGregor whispered back. "This isn't even the frigging start. You ain't seen nuthin yet".

There were yells from the audience: "what is going on? You've taken a wrong turning. We're millions of miles from the Earth". It took five minutes for the captain to calm everyone down. He whispered to Slyme, Trevis and Watts to rush to the control room.

"I honestly don't know what is going on, but we are near the Earth, I assure you we are not anywhere near Saturn. This is some prank, I don't know how it happened. Mr. Sharples, Mr. MacGregor, can you explain all this?"

Both men simply shrugged their shoulders and explained that they were just as baffled as everyone else. Slyme, Trevis and Watts rushed down the auditorium and whispered into Blump's ear.

"Everything is now rectified", said the captain. "It was all some silly joke – nothing more. Anyway, look at the screen. We are now orbiting the Earth. In fifteen minutes we shall land back on good old planet Earth".

The film had indeed been altered and now the audience saw in simulation the Earth getting closer and closer. Soon, there was a shower of dust and everyone saw the familiar inside of the hangar.

Everyone now had their suitcases packed and prepared to assemble at the foyer on the lower deck. Once more, all the crew and staff of the luxury spacecraft were assembled to bid farewell to the passengers.

"Captain, I wonder if we could have a photograph of you, your three senior officers and Dr. Casper Brians in the foyer of the craft?" MacGregor asked Blump. "It would be such a wonderful memento".

"I see no reason as to why not", replied Blump. "It would have to be tomorrow though so as to give Dr. Brians some time to get over here."

"Of course. I'll speak to Dr. Brians when we get back to the Home", MacGregor said.

VII.

Back at the Home, Casper Brians welcomed all his customers back. Everyone assured him that they had enjoyed their long holiday but were unsure as to whether or not they had clinically benefited from the long journey throughout the solar system.

"Could we have a word in private with you, Dr. Brians?" MacGregor asked the asylum governor somewhat discreetly. Brians agreed and he took MacGregor and Sharples to his office.

"So what can I do for you two gentlemen?" asked Brians.

"Well", said MacGregor. "It really was a fantastic simulation of a flight throughout the solar system".

"What are you talking about? What do you mean?" asked Brians.

"Privately, Blump admitted everything to Alfred and me. He said you also knew".

"I see, I see. All right", said Brians collapsing onto his studded leather chair behind his desk. "I did it for the therapeutic benefit of the patients. But I never knew about the fraud".

"Of course you did, Dr. Brians", said Sharples in tones of mock sympathy. "We understand. However, I've arranged with Blump and the others that we have a group photograph at the foyer of the spaceship – tomorrow at 10am".

"Well eh eh you see I'm eh somewhat rather tied up tomorrow and…."

"Tomorrow at 10am sharp", said MacGregor in a low semi-threatening tone.

"And another thing", said MacGregor. "Don't contact Blump or the others between tonight and 10am tomorrow morning. If anything goes amiss, we have someone to contact the police on our behalf."

"And there is just one more task", said Sharples. "Call Bernie Rocks, Reggie Guggins, Pete Proster, Judith Chambers and the other ten members of the Board of *Space Tours, Inc.* We'd like them in the group photo too."

Brians just nodded his head and said, "this is all news to me, I didn't know anything about this con trick".

"I will prove that you did", said MacGregor.

"How? You can't".

"Oh?! Can't I?"

"You have no evidence".

"In good time, Dr. Brians, I will present to you the incontrovertible, undeniable and incontrovertible proof".

Blump and the crew jovially greeted Brians, and the four passengers who had spent three months inside the phony spacecraft. Soon afterwards the 14 member board of *Space Tours, Inc.* arrived and there followed a warm shaking of hands and patting of backs as Rocks and his fellow board members congratulated the bravery and daring of the four passengers in taking such a trip to far off and distant planets. When all this ballyhoo was over, Blump opened the automatic doors of the so-called air-lock.

"You, your crew and your board lead the way, captain, we'll as ever follow after you", said Alfred Sharples.

When the four crew members and the 14 directors were inside the foyer, MacGregor motioning to Brians quietly said "after you Dr. Brians".

Once all the 18 members of *Space Tours, Inc.* were inside the foyer of the craft, MacGregor took out a small remote control device. He pressed one button and the inside doors of the air-lock closed. Then he pressed another button and the outside doors closed.

"What is going on Mr. MacGregor?" asked a somewhat astonished Elizabeth Walters.

"Don't ask questions now", replied Sharples. "All will be revealed to you soon enough".

"In the meantime", said MacGregor, "let's get at least a furlong away from this hangar".

They went outside to where the bus was waiting. Sharples and MacGregor instructed the bus-driver to take them to about a furlong's distance from the hangar. After they alighted from the bus, MacGregor took a computer like contraption out of his rucksack. He set it up on a tripod and began working on it.

"Now look over at the hangar", MacGregor instructed his crew. All of a sudden, there was a tremendous roar from the hangar. The roof was broken and the sides of the hangar started to sway. The five armed guards around the hangar fled for their lives as they realised that the walls were going to give way. Up, up and up went the craft. It soared above the clouds and a few minutes later it disappeared from sight.

"But I thought this thing wasn't a ...." blurted out Sharples. Before he could finish his sentence, MacGregor put the index finger of his right hand to his lips.

"Not now", cautioned MacGregor in a whisper. "Not in front of the bus driver."

"What's going on here?" inquired the bus-driver.

"Oh, we just came to see lift-off", MacGregor informed him. "The company is testing out some new spacecraft systems, so they're taking the craft for a bit of a spin. Just a few orbits around the Earth and home again".

"Yeah, yeah, right".

"What is all this about Mr. MacGregor?" said Susan Blyth. "I thought we were all supposed to line up for a group photograph".

"I'll explain everything back at the nuthouse", said MacGregor. "All aboard the bus for the loony bin", added MacGregor in sarcastic tones.

Back at the asylum MacGregor asked his fellow inmates to assemble in the main lounge where, over coffee and biscuits, he would explain everything. Alfred Sharples, Susan Blyth and Elizabeth Walters, with expressions on their faces which at once betokened anger and bemusement, marched towards the lounge.

Vincent MacGregor started by explaining to them how they had been defrauded. Blyth and Walters were shocked to learn that they had never moved as much as half an inch up into the air let alone having flown to the very edge of the solar system.

"And why are they hurtling about up in space now?" asked Sharples.

"Let's all go to my room. This should all be explained in total confidence and privacy", said MacGregor.

"Now then", continued Dr. Vincent MacGregor, when they were safely ensconced inside his room, "when I had sobered up Mr. Sharples after finding him in a drunken stupor, he asked me why I had been making nightly trips outside the fraudulent spaceship. Well, I was attaching nuclear powered engines to it. I have invented small but extremely powerful engines that can take a massive payload up into space – even something like the windowless hotel we were all imprisoned in for three months. I've now proven that my engines are a success and Blump, Rocks and the others have got more than what they had ever bargained for – they really are in space."

"A nice and ingenious piece of revenge, Dr. MacGregor", said Elizabeth Walters, "but what about our money".

"Do you intend for them to simply perish in space?" asked Susan Blyth. "Although they did the dirty on us, I don't think that mass murder is in order. I'd prefer them to be behind bars and for us to be properly compensated."

MacGregor set up his small portable computer. This time he plugged it into his television set. A minute or so later the crew, the entire Board of *Space Tours, Inc* and Dr. Casper Brians could be seen floating around in what had now become a veritable spacecraft.

VIII.

Speaking into a microphone attached to his computer, Vincent MacGregor addressed the floating fraudsters. "Well, are you having a nice space flight ladies and gentlemen?"

"What the bloody hell is going on Mr. MacGregor?" Rocks yelled out. This was followed by shouts of 'get us down, help help'.

"I can quite easily do that, but first of all, you and your fellow crooks are going to agree to some terms and conditions if you want to remain on the right side of the prison walls".

Screams of 'anything', 'name your terms' 'any price – just get us down' came from the crew and Board.

"Mr. Rocks", MacGregor commenced, "you are going to make a full confession of your fraud which I will record".

"No, no… I …. I can't. Never" Rocks replied.

"No, no, never, then stay in space forever", MacGregor responded in rhythmical tones.

MacGregor then pressed another few buttons. "Very well", he continued. "Now if you look at the monitor which I have re-programmed to show *real* pictures of space, you'll see that I've just sent you on a path which takes you out of Earth orbit. In two days you will be in orbit around the moon. Between now and then, have a sort of board meeting and see if you can din some sense into each other. Bye for now and have a nice flight".

MacGregor then closed down the communications consul and turned to his three friends: "we'll find out in a couple of days whether or not they have seen reason."

Two days later, Blyth, Walters and Sharples entered MacGregor's room to find him getting his communication devices into order. A few minutes later and contact was made with the ship.

"Now", said MacGregor to Rocks who, with the rest of his companions, was floating around in the craft, "are you mugs ready to see reason yet".

"All right", screamed Rocks, "just tell us what you want".

"First of all, a full and unqualified confession made by you on behalf of the entire company".

"Okay", began Rocks, "we perpetrated a fraud on all of you. The craft never went into space and what you and the passengers saw on the monitors was all pre-recorded material."

"And where did you get the recordings from?" Susan Blyth asked.

"We bribed a NASA official to record footage of a real space journey through the solar system. He fitted the spacecraft with a special camera to record everything".

"Who exactly is this NASA official?" Elizabeth Walters asked Rocks.

"Don't answer Rocks", snapped MacGregor. "We don't want this to go public." He then whispered to Elizabeth, "please – for your and the others' benefit, let me ask the questions".

"Now", pleaded Rocks, "can you bring us back to Earth?"

"Not quite yet", responded MacGregor. "We are going to hammer out a little business arrangement between your board and our board".

"What board?"

"We have formed ourselves into a company called *Solar System Holidays*. I am the Chairman of the Board, Mr. Sharples here is Director of Operations and Supplies. Mrs. Elizabeth Walters is Personnel Director and Miss Susan Blyth is Director of Tours."

"I am not a mere Personnel Director", objected Elizabeth. "I am the Empress of the Company".

"Very well", sighed MacGregor, "then Empress of the Company you shall be". Sharples and Blyth looked at each other and smiled; even Rocks and some of his companions managed a titter or two even though by now the condition on the spaceship was becoming somewhat bleak. The oxygen supply was running low and it was hard to rustle up anything more than a sandwich in zero gravity.

"Down to business", snapped MacGregor. "You are going to give each of us 100,000 pounds. That is, 40,000 pounds as a refund and 60,000 pounds as compensation. Then you are going to agree to a merger between *Space Tours, Inc.* and *Solar System Holidays*.

You are going to fit up your phony craft with my new nuclear powered spacecraft engines. I'm setting up my own personal business *MacGregor Space Engines and Space Systems* and you're going to buy exclusively from me".

At this point Susan Blyth intervened. "And, Mr. Rocks, you are going to buy all your provisions from me. You'll buy your foodstuffs from *Blyth Catering Ltd.* I have the monopoly on that."

"And as for alcoholic beverages, my houses of refreshment have the monopoly, eh Mr. Rocks?" said Alfred Sharples.

"My husband Napoleon Bonaparte has an interior decorating company. The Emperor and Empress command that you do provide exclusive rights for us to furnish your spacecraft-hotel".

"Profits from *Space Tours, Inc* and *Solar System Holidays* will be split 50/50 – straight down the middle", said MacGregor.

"I don't know if we can accept all that?" said Rocks somewhat despondingly. "Can we have an hour to discuss it?"

"Yes", replied MacGregor impatiently. "You have one hour – starting 55 minutes ago. I'll give you two choices if you refuse this offer: I'll bring you back to Earth where you can face arrest, trial and incarceration; or I'll set you on a course for Mars. Take your pick ladies and gentlemen".

"We accept, we accept", shouted Rocks and the rest of the board and crew of *Space Tours, Inc*. "Just get us home – get us back to Earth".

"All right", said MacGregor. "I'm now setting you on a course for Earth. And by the way, when you return to Earth, don't renege on the bargain as this deal as well as your confession has been recorded. Renege on it and we'll hand you over to the Fraud Squad. Now to turn to you Dr. Brians."

"Why do you involve me in all of this?" protested Brians. "I have no holdings at all in *Space Tours, Inc.*"

"No, but you are an accomplice in this fraud, nevertheless".

"I deny that totally. That is pure slander Mr. MacGregor".

"It's Dr. MacGregor if you don't mind. Now Mr. Rocks, did you pay Brians any commission?"

"Absolutely not", blurted out Rocks.

"You have no evidence", screamed Brians.

"Oh haven't I?" said MacGregor as he inserted what appeared like a small chip into his computer. He then invited Rocks and his associates to look at the monitor in front of them.

Here is what they saw: Brians heard his own voice coming back at him. "Very well, but a few minutes only. Five to be precise and starting two minutes ago."

"You see Dr. Brians", said Rocks, "the spacecraft will never leave the Earth. The passengers will merely enter a windowless hotel designed like a spaceship. What they will see during their three months stay will merely be pre-recorded footage of the solar system."

"But this is highly fraudulent, Mr. Rocks".

"But perhaps highly therapeutic, Dr. Brians."

"A windowless hotel! And how are the inmates going to breathe?"

"There will be a regular supply of oxygen pumped into the building".

"Well, I'm not sure if we can go along with this".

"'We',Dr. Brians. Who is this 'we'?"

"Surely I will have to consult one or two colleagues as to the efficacy of all of this".

"Dr. Brians. Let's just keep this between you and me and the Board. Shall we say five percent of the fare?"

"Em – I'd prefer ten percent".

"Eight percent?"

"Done".

The DVD presentation came to an end. Rocks and Brians looked positively ill.

"How did you record all this, you weren't even in the room?" said Brians

"That's academic and irrelevant", said MacGregor calmly. "The fact is I have it recorded. But to satisfy your curiosity, I planted a nano camera in your office. I've not only recorded this crooked deed with Rocks but a few other things such as your secret tippling. Yes, you have a bit of a drink problem, Brians".

"All right, all right, I admit I made a deal with Rocks", said Brians.

"Now then, Dr. Brians", MacGregor continued firmly, "we want you to recommend *Space Tours, Inc* and *Solar System Holidays* to your patients. And we want ten percent of the profits from your *Home of Relaxation for the Mentally Il- at- Ease.*"

Brians nodded consent. He was in a state of severe shock. All he really wanted now was to get back to Earth and stay out of jail. Brians and the others realised that all the money in the world was completely and utterly worthless away from Earth. 'You can't take it with you when you go', was an adage which seemed to them to take on a more tangible meaning. There was no greater likelihood of pockets in a spacesuit than there were in a shroud. And there were definitely no ATMs in space!

Two days later the spacecraft landed. Brians, Rocks and the others staggered out of the craft coughing and spluttering and gasping for air. When everyone was assembled on the open field where the hangar had once stood, Alfred Sharples took a much closer look at one of the Board members. There was something familiar about her. It dawned on Alfred who she was; and it dawned on Jennifer Low who he was. How old, wrinkled and bossy she looked. And how potbellied, balding and bleary-eyed he looked. Both pretended not to have recognised each other. MacGregor then told Rocks that the *Space Tours, Inc.* would be meeting with the legal teams of the various businesses mentioned during the Earth to spacecraft negotiations. They would hammer out the new contractual arrangements between and among the various parties. How diminished would Jennifer Low's financial situation now become, how enhanced would Alfred Sharples' become. Jennifer knew this and Alfred knew this. Jennifer looked at Alfred again and walked over to him.

"Oh Alfred", Jennifer started off, "is it really you? Oh this is like a dream come true. I think it's now time for me to stop playing so hard to get. I just overdid it I guess. Anyway, here I am now Alfred, ready to start our lives together."

Alfred Sharples, without even looking at Jennifer Low simply replied – "sod off".

THE DIMRUN HOTEL.

I.

In the Lancashire town of Krowbar stood the 130 room Dimrun Hotel. At best, you could say that this was a zero star category hotel. When you walked into the foyer of this establishment, you were at once greeted by the dark brown wood paneling of imitation mahogany that made up most of its interior design. The faded carpets, the threadbare curtains hiding the cracked glass of the foyer windows and the peeling wallpaper between the depressing dark panels did nothing to lift the spirits and gladden the hearts of the diminishing number of patrons who, from time to time, still frequented the Dimrun Hotel. This threadbare, fading, depressing and gloomy scene was well matched by the equally threadbare, fading, depressing and gloomy manager, the pompous, humourless, stuffed-shirt, bubble brain Mr. Nelson Dateland Walkees. Oh indeed – the Dimrun Hotel had seen better days – especially when Dateland Walkees was not the manager. Now to be fair to old Walkees, it wasn't entirely his fault; the hotel used to cater to the owners and managers of the massive factories and sweat-shops which the Industrial Revolution had thrown up in Krowbar. Post-industrial Britain was a different story though. Heavy

37

industry was gone, Krowbar's port was a decaying mass of rusting metal and ruined warehouses. So the Dimrun Hotel which had once thrived on businessmen using its facilities for conferences and business luncheons, or in providing rooms for the visiting delegations of industrialists who came from every corner of the world to purchase the produce of Krowbar, now pinned its hopes on at least some of the town's inhabitants spending a part of their Giro cheques on tea and muffins in the ground floor coffee shop. Few however were going for the buffets and 'special offers' with which the Dimrun tried to entice customers. And the Board of Directors of the Dimrun Hotel were not going for the excuses of the worst manager they had ever employed.

Mr. Michael Dimrun and his seven member board knew they were scraping the bottom of the barrel when they took on Nelson Dateland Walkees, but real hotel managers had moved off to better pastures. They went to London, the States or to places like Dubai and Abu Dhabi where they could make it big time and use their managerial skills and talents to the fullest extent, so the likes of the Dimrun had to fall back on the Dateland Walkees of the world of hotel management (mismanagement). "We're left with the useless shite like Dateland Walkess", Mr. Dimrun used to say to his fellow board members when he was perusing the ever narrowing profit margins of the hotel. Mrs. Dorothy Dimrun wondered as to whether or not Dateland Walkees was embezzling. Her husband dismissed this, not because of any virtues imputed to Dateland Walkees but simply on the grounds that he did not have the intelligence.

II.

Nelson Dateland Walkees had been summoned to appear before the entire Board of Directors of the Dimrun Hotel.

"Yes, yes, yes", said Michael Dimrun, "you've made that plea many times before Mr. Walkees, we know all about the industrial decline of Krowbar. But it's not the entire story."

"But I'm doing everything I can, Mr. Dimrun sir", whimpered Walkees.

"That is not the opinion of my fellow board members and I".

"There is nothing more I can do".

"That also is not the collective opinion of the Board".

"So what am I supposed to do?"

"We need results Mr. Walkees, results".

"Results?"

"Yes Mr. Walkees, results".

"But I cannot reverse the fortunes of an entire town".

"No, but you can reverse the fortunes of this hotel. You must do something imaginative, you must be creative. Above all, you must adapt to changing circumstances. You are not doing any of these things. In fact, you can't even use a computer."

"You mean those things with the big whirring tapes?"

"No, no Walkees. They sit on your desk. You can even carry them around – these are called laptops. In fact, you can even access the internet on some mobile 'phones. Now I've heard you've been having trouble with your office 'phone and your car"

"I can't find the cranking handles for either of them".

The members of the board looked at each other with incredulity. A few seconds later there were suppressed titters and sniggers around the boardroom table. Mr. Dimrun then looked serious again and he looked seriously at Walkees.

"Mr. Walkees, we are going to give you six weeks to turn this hotel around. Six weeks, Mr. Walkees, six weeks. And if we do not see an improvement, then Mr. Walkees, you will be going walkies!"

III.

So poor old Walkees walked gloomily back to his gloomy and dingy office in his gloomy and dingy hotel. He turned up the lighting in his office by adjusting the gas mantel above his desk. He just didn't know what to do? He ordered a cup of tea (and paid for it) and then started thumbing through the newspapers. There was nothing there which in any way could have given him inspiration, the news was as bad as his hotel: another strike, another factory closure, more layoffs, then Harold Shipman and other criminals. And the sports pages didn't offer the poor dunderhead much consolation either, well, a little perhaps; his team, the Lancashire Louts had been promoted to the 7th Division.

That night, Dateland Walkees tossed and turned in his bed. He had dreams of Giro cheques and joblessness. But there was one dream that caused him to suddenly wake up and sit up in bed. He was in a cold sweat and he was shaking with fear. He lit the gas mantel but this only served to increase his fears as the shadows cast by its yellowish flame seemed to give substance to the horrific imagery of the nightmare from which he had just awoken. It was something he had read in the newspaper. He had only skimmed through its pages and had never really absorbed anything of its contents. Somehow or other though, an article from that paper must have stuck in his mind and played upon his depressed condition by developing the ghastly scenario that proceeded from the sewers of his demented sub-conscious. And now the horror seemed to play itself out in the dancing shadows from the flickering gas light.

Something drew Walkees' attention to the gas flame. For some unknown reason, he just kept staring at it. The flame started to get brighter. For a few moments, Walkees watched in fascination. The flame continued to glow in brightness until the room was enveloped in an intense white light. By now, Dateland Walkees was paralysed with utter terror. He passed out and fell into a deep sleep.

Walkees woke up the next morning feeling amazingly refreshed. The sun was shining through his window and through the worn old curtains which were drawn in front of it. The light from the sun did not have to struggle too hard to find its way into Walkees' room. He looked out at the familiar scene from his bedroom window – the ill-kept and unswept streets, the dilapidated buildings, the derelict factories, the condemned dwelling places of Krowbar's yesteryear – such was the view of decay which greeted the eyes of the hotel manager each morning. Yet, in spite of this picture of depression, in spite of the nightmare he had experienced, Walkees felt in great spirits. He could not understand why, but he understood that a new vitality was surging through his entire being, a whole new lease of life had been given to him and, most of all, he knew exactly what he was going to do to turn the hotel around.

IV.

Two months later and the fortunes of the Dimrun Hotel were being turned around. Walkees had beef from the African country of Bongaland specially flown in for the Friday brunches he had started offering at his hotel. He had done some research into the kinds of beef from various countries. Well, he had got others to do the research for him as the dimwitted dunderhead didn't know how to use a computer. And, being the knuckle-dragger that he was, he didn't even know how to switch on a computer; in fact, the poor old aging dunce didn't even know what computers were for! Nevertheless, in spite of the astronomically high costs of having this meat flown in all the way from Africa, the Dimrun debts were being discharged and a profit was beginning to show.

"I'm actually a vegetarian Walkees", said Mr. Michael Dimrun, "but I understand that there is something very special about this meat. Tell me Walkees, what exactly is it that gives Bongaland beef its unique taste?"

"Well, Mr. Dimrun sir, it's the sort of African grass that the cows are fed on. Also, once the cattle are slaughtered, the meat is treated with a special something-or-other."

"A special something-or-other, Mr. Walkees?" said Dimrun in puzzled and inquisitive tones. "Whatever do you mean? What exactly is this 'something-or-other'?"

"Well, I eh, erm, I don't really know. It's em, it's..... a secret".

"All right then Walkees. Now, what the Board and I find somewhat strange is the mathematics of all of this".

"But I don't understand maths", pleaded Walkees.

"Of course you don't Walkees, but we do. The cost of the beef over the takings from the Friday brunches has been insufficient to have covered all the debt that the hotel ran up over the last few years. Yet, not only have you discharged the debt, but even produced a small profit".

"I, I, I, can explain all that", stammered Walkees. "You see, so many of the wealthy businessmen have been so pleased with the meat – they say it's the best they've ever tasted, that they have given large donations, just out of sheer gratitude. So I've been using these donations to pay off the hotel's debts."

"All right then Mr. Walkees. Money is money and it doesn't really matter where it comes from or why people give us it".

"The customers are very grateful, Mr. Dimrun"

"Yes of course they are Walkees, and for that matter, so am I. However, Mr. Walkees, we must do more. We are making a profit, thanks to you, but it is barely above break-even. We must try harder Mr. Walkees."

"What would you like me to do, Mr. Dimrun?"

"One of the waiters -that man", said Dimrun pointing to a waiter. The waiter was small in stature and walked with a kind of stoop.

"We don't know his name but we call him Uriah Heep. Everyone talks about how creepy he is. In fact, he's even more obsequious than you are Walkees. Do something about it, Walkees, do something. We don't want creeps among the staff at this hotel".

Mr. Dimrun went out of the restaurant and Mr. Walkees went up to Uriah. "I heard, Mr. Heep, I heard that rumour has it that yesterday afternoon someone crept. Now it wasn't Mr. Dimrun, it wasn't me, it wasn't the head waiter, it wasn't any member of the Board   it was you Heep, it was you wasn't it. Come on own up, Heep. It was you."

"But Mr. General Manager, sir, I was hoping that my creeping would be up to a better standard by now".

"We have been watching you of late Heep. All this creeping, all this creeping. And not only creeping but crawling, pandering, flattering, sniveling, groveling, kowtowing - and I believe that you've even added bowing and scraping to your repertoire. Well, we just can't have it, it's all going to stop you know Heep."

Having watched all this were two individuals. They were simply known as 'the man in the pin-stripped suit' and 'the man in the dickie bow tie'. Both worked at reception, and both were in competition with Uriah Heep as to who was the biggest creep of all. Such was the high level of creeping that Uriah Heep had attained through years of experience in the art that the man in the pin-striped suit and the man in the dickie bow tie decided not to compete against each other in the obsequiousness stakes; instead they would team up, and so, with their combined efforts, they would try to overtake Heep as the chief creep.

Walkees had mixed feelings as he sat in his office. He was happy that Michael Dimrun had been pleased with his efforts. Yet, he knew that he had to do better still. Without fully being aware of it, Walkees was staring at the flame of the gas mantel in his office. It grew brighter and brighter, changing from the usual dull yellow to the whiter than white light so unusual in such a device. Walkees then had another brilliant idea. He called the Executive Chef, Mr. Dermot Pans, into his office.

"You wanted to see me about something Mr. Walkees", said the Executive Chef as he entered the GM's office.

"Ah, Mr. Pans, do come in", replied Walkees. "Now I understand that you are the Executive Chef in this hotel".

"Yes, that's right. Have been for the past ten years".

"Well, the question I want to ask you is this, Mr. Pans: what exactly do you execute?"

"You know, I execute orders to my kitchen staff. I execute orders to the hotel's suppliers."

"It doesn't sound too convincing to me Mr. Pans. It doesn't seem to warrant the title 'executive'".

"I do everything that most executive chefs do, Mr. Walkees. What more can I do that would, well, that would be 'executive'?"

"You see, Mr. Pans, any Tom, Dick or Harry can order food or tell others how to cook it. That wouldn't exactly make them an 'executive'".

"Mr. Walkees, I wonder if you could get to the point of all this. What exactly are you getting at?"

"It is this. I intend to change your title. As you know, I have been given a brief by the hotel's Board to be imaginative and creative so as to attract clientele to this establishment. If you are not executing anything then you cannot keep the title of Executive Chef."

"So are you demoting me, Mr. Walkees. If you are, then you will simply have to replace me. The new Executive Chef will be doing neither more nor less than I am".

"No, Mr. Pans, I am neither promoting nor demoting you. Your title is to be changed from the Executive Chef to the Executed Chef".

"A rose by any other name, Mr. Walkees. I cannot see how that can be considered as 'imaginative' or 'creative.'"

"You haven't heard everything yet, Mr. Pans. You haven't heard exactly what the creative act is in which I intend to engage."

"And what precisely is that, Mr. Walkees? Could you spell it out please?"

"It is this Mr. Pans. We are going to execute you."

"I beg your pardon".

"You heard what I said".

Pans had a somewhat startled look on his face. After he had recovered from this bizarre announcement, his shock gave way to merriment – he simply burst out laughing. "Walkees, you've gone off your rocker. You're as mad as a hatter. You can't be serious".

"Oh really. Look at this hype I've put in the newspapers".

Dermot Pans took the newspaper out of Dateland Walkees' hand. He read the large advertisement under Classifieds. 'Come to the Dimrun Hotel and see the Executive Chef being executed. This is a once-off event of course so don't miss it. We'll start with some live entertainment followed by a buffet dinner. And the grand finale will be when our Executive Chef is led out blind folded. A six-man firing squad will then execute the Executive Chef.'

"We really have to shoot you, Pans", said Walkees. "I've already hired the firing squad so I have to pay them whether you are executed or not. So, we get our money's worth and execute you".

"Most of us at this Hotel have you down as a bit of a dunce Walkees, but this time you've really shown yourself to be prime for the nuthouse."

With that, Dermot Pans stormed out of Walkees' office. As he approached the lifts, he noticed two figures near the offices which were a little way off from Walkees' office. He looked at them, and the man in the pin striped suit and the man in the dicky bow tie looked at him. As Pans looked at these two, he shook his head in exasperation; but they just looked as stiff, and as pompous and as obsequious as ever. "What a pair of creeps!" thought Pans to himself.

V.

One evening, at around 11pm, Nelson Dateland Walkees was inspecting the coffee shop. He noticed that the tables had already been set out for breakfast. Three waiters were standing at the check-out counter. They were busy adding up the day's takings and squaring the cash with the accounts. Walkees however espied a fourth waiter in the coffee-shop, he was just adding the finishing touches to one of the tables in the corner of the room. It was Uriah Heep.

"Who has laid all these tables for breakfast?" asked Walkees as he looked at the three waiters at the check-out desk.

All at once, Uriah started to get excited. Bobbing up and down he answered the manager's question with, "me, me, me, Mr. General Manager sir. See, see, I did well, yes?"

Walkees merely looked at his watch with a somewhat puzzled expression on his countenance. He then looked at the coffee shop clock and back at his watch again. The puzzlement continued as he looked at the tables and then again at his watch. "Brrrrrreakfast", Walkees blurted out. "Brrrreakfast?" he repeated. Walkees then put the index finger of his right hand on the side of his chin and kept repeating the same word in quick succession – "breakfast – breakfast, breakfast, breakfast." He then hesitated for a moment. The look of bewilderment left his face and Walkees appeared sensible – well as sensible as he ever could be. "No", he snapped. "We can't have it. Breakfast things on the table at 11 o'clock at night?! We just can't have it. Heep, you must prepare the tables at the appointed times for meals. Really", continued Walkees indignantly, "breakfast things out at 11 o'clock at night. Clear those things away Heep", said the manager pointing at the tables. "Breakfast things at this time of night? That's real creepiness. Only a right creep would do a thing like that".

Poor Uriah Heep, he had to go and undo all the things he had done over the past hour. As Uriah dismantled the breakfast appurtenances from the tables of the coffee shop, the manager stood watching him with rapid nodding movements of the head in mock and sarcastic approval.

When the harassed waiter had finished taking all the breakfast crockery and cutlery off the table, he stood stooped in front of Walkees who, calmly pointing to a trolley near the check-out said " put them ....over there". And as Uriah did so, the mock approval nodding started up again.

Walkees then left the coffee shop. Outside of the coffee shop looking on were the man in the pin striped suit and the man in the dicky bow tie. "What a pair of dimwits", thought Walkees to himself.

And so it came to pass that the day for Dermot Pans' execution had arrived. The hotel was jam packed. Everyone enjoyed a good meal and were entertained with live bands, singers and various performers.

"And now for the moment you've all been waiting for", bellowed out Walkees, "the execution of our Executive Chef".

Dermot Pans was led out by the major who would give the orders for the firing squad. The six member firing squad walked behind the major and the chef. Neither the major nor his soldiers looked particularly steady on their feet. Pans started walking in a circle. The major and his soldiers yelled at him asking him to stand still. They followed him as he ran and after a few minutes they were even more unsteady on their feet. Eventually Pans managed to get them to stand in a circle. Pans stood in the middle, the major outside of the circle. The major then gave the order to aim. When he yelled "fire", Pans ducked down. The shots rang out and the six soldiers fell dead.

The reaction from the guests was mixed. Most of them thought it was quite amusing that the members of the execution squad had executed each other. A few however were not impressed. "Mr. Walkees, we came here to see the chef being executed, not the firing squad", commented one guest. The man in the pin striped suit and the man in the dicky bow tie watched all the guests as they walked out of the hotel.

The next morning, no less a personage than Mrs. Dorothy Dimrun came in for breakfast. Uriah Heep was at his most obsequious. As she was about to leave, a lady walked in. Mrs. Dimrun and the lady were friends and they started talking. After a few minutes, Mrs. Dimrun's ten year old daughter started tugging at her mother's sleeve.

"Oh what is it?" asked Mrs. Dimrun in rather annoyed tones. "Can't you see I'm talking to Mrs. Fyfe-Bradley?"

"But mummy, mummy!" said the little girl equally annoyed and with her hands on her hips, "Heep's creeping again".

"Ohhhhh give it up Heep", said Mrs. Dimrun in a disgusted way, "finish it off, end it all".

A few minutes more and the little girl was once more tugging at her mother's sleeve.

"Oh what is it now?" asked Dorothy Dimrun impatiently.

"But actually mummy, Heep's still creeping".

Mrs. Dimrun looked over to the waiter and simply said "oh give it up Heep".

Almost needless to say, the man in the pin striped suit and the man in the dicky bow tie observed it all.

"Now just what happened last night?" Mr. Dimrun angrily asked Walkees. "The Chef is still alive, he is still unexecuted. It's just not good enough".

"I spoke to Pans about it. It appears, Mr. Dimrun sir, that Pans treated the major and his firing squad to drinks before the execution was due to take place. They just had one too many. Then, with Pans running around in a circle, they were completely bambozzled. So they ended up executing each other instead of the executed chef."

"Will you be trying this line again?"

"Oh indeed. We'll try again next Tuesday evening".

"Would you and your men like a drink, Major?" asked Walkees the following Tuesday evening.

"Aw huh huh huh no Mr. Pans. You're not going to catch me falling for that trick a second time.

Once the festivities were over, Pans was led out by a stone cold sober firing squad. He was blindfolded and the order was given by the major – first to aim, then to fire. The soldiers discharged their guns but Pans simply stood there. He was as alive as alive could be.

"Ha ha", laughed Pans. "You see I made myself a bullet proof vest from the kitchenware."

"All right Major. Take that bullet proof vest off of him and go through the execution procedures again".

"Mmm well eh no Mr. Walkees", replied the major. "You have only paid for one execution ceremony. And in any case, my men only took one bullet each".

The guests left the hotel shaking their heads and shrugging their shoulders while the man in the pin striped suit and the man in the dicky-bow tie looked on.

"You know Walkees", said Mr. Dimrun, "this is the second time you have fouled up."

"I'll try to do better the next time, Mr. Dimrun."

"How on earth did I ever choose such a boneheaded manager?" asked Mr. Dimrun of himself.

VI.

"Mr. Walkees, may I have a little word with you"? Uriah Heep asked the manager when he visited the coffee-shop on his daily inspection rounds of the hotel.

"Yes what is it Heep? Has it anything to do with your creeping?"

"Yes indeed it has Mr. General Manager sir".

"There you go again Heep, creeping and crawling. If you really must behave in this obsequious way, at least make sure that your creeping is up to standard."

Walkees and Heep went off to the GM's office and spoke for a good half hour. At the end of the meeting, Walkees was quite shaken but Heep looked rather pleased with himself. Later that day, Mrs. Dorothy Dimrun came into the coffee-shop with a proposal for Heep.

"Well Mr. Heep, we are thinking of transferring you to our restaurant near the beach. Would you like to go?"

"Not really Mrs. Dimrun Ma'am. I think I'd rather stay here."

"There'll be a lot of opportunities for creeping", Mrs. Dimrun assured him.

"No, I think I'd prefer to do my creeping here, if you don't mind. Anyway I do have a counter-proposal to put to the hotel but I don't want to do it right away. You see Mrs. Dimrun I'm ever so humble."

"And when do you intend to put this counter-proposal to us Mr. Heep? When will you tell Mr. Dimrun about it?"

"You see, I'm a very humble man, Mrs. Dimrun, so I'll put my proposal to Mr. Walkees a little later."

That evening, as Walkees closed the door of his room in the GM's living quarters of the hotel, he was exhausted after the day's exertions. Just as he was about to lie down he heard a soft tap on the door. "Who is it?" he called out.

"Oh Mr. General Manager", hissed the voice from outside the room.

"Yes Heep?" said Walkees.

"About that demotion that I've always wanted".

"It's being taken care of".

"Oh and Mr. General Manager".

"Yes Heep".

"That salary decrease that I put in for some time ago".

"I'll see to it right away Heep."

"Mr. General Manager", hissed Heep one more time.

"Yes Heep".

But Heep said nothing. He simply crept away from the General Manager's room, down to the hotel lobby. How Heep's obsequious stooping posture blended well with the dark and dingy imitation mahogany wood paneling of the dreary lobby. Heep crept out of the hotel room, cringed before some guests who were just arriving and then crawled off home. Observing Mr. Heep creeping along the street were the man in the pin striped suit and the man in the dicky bow tie.

Walkees managed to persuade Mr. Dimrun to allow him to have just one more go at executing the chef.

"Now then", said Mr. Dimrun on the night of the execution. "You've checked everything is in order".

"Yes", Walkees reassured his boss.

"The major and his firing squad are all sober?"

"Check – affirmative".

"Pans isn't sporting a bullet proof vest?"

"Check – affirmative".

So, once again, Pans was brought out for execution. The major gave the orders to his men. They raised their rifles and on the commanded from the major, opened fire on

Pans. Immediately they did so, they all staggered backwards clutching their chests after which they immediately fell to the ground dead.

"That's 12 men now I've lost because of your bumbling idiocy Walkees. You're going to pay for this, you dumb ass."

"How did this happen?" Mr. Dimrun asked Walkees the next day.

"Mr. Dimrun, it's something I just could never have foreseen. I questioned Pans on it and he told me that he has this scientist friend who has been working on a new type of bullet proof vest. Not only does it stop the bullets, it actually causes them to rebound. That's why the soldiers in the firing squad died."

"We had been thinking of sacking you Walkees, but in spite of the heavy payments connected to the execution debacle, we are still making good profits from your Bongaland meat."

"Thank you Mr. Dimrun."

"Now there is another matter I'd like to bring up Mr. Walkees."

"Yes Mr. Dimrun?"

"You have been spending a lot of time away from the hotel since you embarked on these projects."

"Well I have been going out personally promoting these buffets and other events. Advertising in the papers and through the internet is one thing, but there is still nothing like the good old-fashioned personal touch."

"But I've been noticing that you have been attending a lot of funerals lately. I hope Walkees that you are not doing professional mourning on the side."

"Oh no! When any of our elderly patrons die, we want to ensure that their surviving relatives continue their patronage of the Dimrun Hotel."

"All right Walkees. As long as it keeps the customers rolling in. But, Mr. Walkees, no creeping please. It's bad enough that we already have one creep in the hotel."

"Oh ah, eh you mean the waiter that everyone calls Uriah Heep."

"Yes indeed. Now Walkees, you don't seem to have managed to contain his creeping. If anything, it's been getting worse of late."

"Worse Mr. Dimrun?"

"Yes, worse Mr. Walkees", hollered Dimrun.

"Well it's not very easy dealing with such an individual, Mr. Dimrun sir".

"Do something about it Walkees, do something about it".

"Well, I'm trying, my best, really I am."

"Try a bit harder Mr. Walkees, try a bit harder."

Dateland Walkees left the boardroom and went back to his own office. Near the lifts he noticed the man in the pin striped suit and the man in the dicky bow tie. Walkees was in a foul sort of mood after his interview with Dimrun. He blurted out at the two hotel employees – "what a pair of creeps you are, get rid of that obsequious pompous Jeeves look".

In unison, the man in the pin striped suit and the man in the dicky bow tie simply gave out a long dreary butler-like "very good sir".

"Gawwwwd", blurted out Walkees. What a pair of creepy crawlies you two are."

Once back in his office Walkees started to reflect on how things had developed recently. "Uriah Heep the creep knows what I'm up to. Now as for those two knuckle-heads in the pin striped suit and the dicky bow tie – they don't know anything and are unlikely to, they're simply too bloody stupid. Obsequious and stupid, that's what those two are

– obsequious and stupid. And I'm not sure if they're more obsequious than stupid or more stupid than obsequious. Whatever it is, my secret is safe. I don't have to worry about those two numbskulls."

VII.

"So what's this new idea of yours, Walkees? I hope it's better than the 'executed chef' stunt".

"It's an Indian restaurant Mr. Dimrun. I think an Indian restaurant would attract a lot of people."

"But Krowbar already is well enough endowed with Indian restaurants, Mr. Walkees. They are long established, serve first class Indian food and are very popular. I don't think we could compete, quite honestly".

"I've hired an Indian to run it Mr. Dimrun. His name is Arup Kumar Singh Deo. He has some brilliant ideas which he says will make the Dimrun Indian restaurant unique among all the Indian restaurants in Krowbar.

"All right Walkees. I'll put it to my fellow board members and see what they have to say about it."

A few days later Walkees was called to the boardroom where Mr. Dimrun was waiting to see him.

"You wanted to see me Mr. Dimrun sir", said Walkees somewhat obsequiously.

"Yes, come in Walkees, kneel…. eh I mean, sit down. Well Dateland Walkess, your idea for an Indian restaurant has been approved by the Board. Now when does Mr. Arup Kumar Singh Deo arrive from India?"

"He said he is ready to come at any time."

"Very well, Walkees; now your brief is this: we'll turn over some of the vacant office rooms in the lobby for your

Indian restaurant. Renovation and reconstruction work will begin immediately. As soon as your Mr. Singh Deo arrives get cracking on the menu."

One month later, the Indian restaurant was ready. At first it did very well, but after a while it started to go downhill.

"Well Mr. Arup Kumar Singh Deo", said Walkees, "your menu doesn't seem to be attracting the customers. Why are they not coming back? I think it was just the novelty of a new restaurant that accounted for its initial success. Now Mr. Singh Deo, we need to do something to entice the customers back."

"I think we need to make the food more spicy", replied Singh Deo. "The main problem with the other Indian restaurants in Krowbar is that their food isn't spicy enough".

"We'll give it a try then. Let's see if spicier food brings the customers flocking back".

"Could we possibly call one of our new dishes 'nincompoop'?"

"Why on earth would you want to call it that, Mr. Singh Deo?"

"In your honour, Mr. Walkees".

"I beg your pardon", said Walkees quite taken aback. "Where did you get this idea from?"

"It was just the other day – when Mr. Dimrun was complimenting you", answered Singh Deo with total innocence.

"Well, I can't possibly have a dish named after me – certainly not with that name?"

"Oh, you're far too modest Mr. Walkees".

So the weeks rolled by, but Singh Deo's spicier dishes did not seem to do the magic. The customers were just not coming to the Indian restaurant at the Dimrun Hotel.

Singh Deo's response was simply to make the food spicier and spicier.

"Mr. Dimrun is getting really impatient with us Arup. He says he's only going to give us two more weeks to buck up or he'll close down the restaurant."

Out of sheer desperation, Singh Deo trebled the amount of the special spices he had brought with him from India. Only one customer had come to try out Singh Deo's latest 'speciality of the house'. Walkees and Singh Deo watched the man as he ate the very spicy chicken and rice dish.

"How is the food sir?" asked Singh Deo.

The man did not reply. He simply grew redder and redder in the face. His mouth was tightly closed.

"Is everything all right?" Walkees asked the solitary customer. Again, the man did not reply. His faced just continued to go redder by the second. He stood up, and, as he did so, smoke started billowing out of his ears. He ran to the door, opened it and darted out onto the pavement. Walkees and Singh Deo ran after him. What happened next convinced them that they must have been dreaming. The customer opened his mouth and all of a sudden fire belched out from it. But there were more surprises in store; the man started to ascend upwards, fire coming out of not only his mouth but his behind. Up, up, up and away he went until he was totally out of sight. Walkees and Singh Deo just stared at each other in complete and utter disbelief.

"That does it", screamed Michael Dimrun, "that bloody well does it. The Indian restaurant is closing. Do you know that this hotel is known as 'the hotel of death' because of you two?"

"But we can't be sure if the spices are to blame for this freak event", pleaded Singh Deo.

In a fit of uncontrollable temper, Dimrun ran into the kitchen and took all the bottles of Singh Deo's spices and smashed them on the pavement outside the hotel. The cats, dogs, mice and rats from the alleyways near the hotel dashed towards this most unexpected free meal awaiting them on the pavement. A few minutes later, like the customer of the previous evening, fire came out of their mouths and backsides and up they went to join the customer in orbit.

A bellboy came into the restaurant to announce a visitor who requested the pleasure of the company of Mr. Michael Dimrun and Mr. Nelson Dateland Walkees. Dimrun and Walkees went out into the lobby to greet their visitor.

Presenting what appeared like an ID card of some description, the visitor said "good morning, I'm Chief Inspector Charles Evens from CID."

"Good morning Chief Inspector", said Dimrun, "what can we do for you?"

"Would one of you two gentlemen happen to be Mr. Nelson Dateland Walkees?"

"I am", replied Walkees.

"Mr. Walkees, we have an arrest warrant for you. Would you please come with us sir? You are to be charged with multiple acts of murder."

Down at the police station, Chief Inspector Evens was busily engaged in the interrogation of his suspect.

"We have noticed a consistent pattern in the deaths of these people", said Evens. "They have all died of salmonella poisoning. And they all frequented the Dimrun Hotel's Friday brunches."

"But that doesn't prove it was me. You will need more evidence than that, Chief Inspector".

"Oh we have it Walkees, we have it. We have been in close co-operation with the police in Bongaland and they have inspected all shipments of beef ordered by your hotel. They have been found to be completely free of salmonella. Now when they have been offloaded from the cargo plane at Blackpool Airport these shipments have been trucked not directly to the Dimrun Hotel but to the agricultural research station where your accomplice Dr. Harry Skipman treated them with salmonella."

"And what in blue blazes would be my motive for wanting to quite literally kill off the hotel's clientele?"

"I'm just coming to that, Mr. Walkees. We have been doing some research at the Wills and Probate Office and we have discovered that large legacies were provided for you and Dr. Skipman by the deceased. We have arrested Dr. Skipman and he has confessed to everything. Further police investigation has shown that you paid off the hotel debts with the money from these legacies."

"Why would I personally want to pay off the debts of a hotel which I do not own?" protested Walkees.

"Because these debts were run up by you, Mr. Walkees. Had the hotel gone into receivership, your embezzlement would have been discovered. You see one of your waiters known as Uriah Heep found out quite recently about your fiddling. He's such a creep that he literally crept up behind you while you were cooking the books and noted everything. In fact this man is such a creep that he could stand behind you for hours on end and you wouldn't even know he was there. He has been arrested on a charge of blackmail. He was actually recorded on DVD blackmailing you. The price for his silence was your acquiescence in his creeping. All of that was caught on DVD too. Dimrun and his Board thought you weren't clever enough to fiddle, but Heep realised that you weren't quite that much of a fat-head."

"Who sent you the DVD? Who made these recordings?"

"We don't know quite frankly. That's a mystery, but we have these recordings. They were sent to us anonymously. The Dimrun's books have been obtained under a subpoena and they clearly show your embezzlement and the subsequent covering up of it."

"If the deceased persons you refer to wanted to leave me money, then that surely is their business. I cannot force anyone to write out a will in my favour."

"Well you couldn't Mr. Walkees – you're clever enough; but Dr. Harry Skipman is. He injected his patients with a substance that frazzled their brains to such an extent that they became amenable to anything suggested to them. Dr. Skipman has confessed everything. Laboratory analysis of the salmonella that you and Skipman put in the meat shows that the salmonella was treated with a substance that at once covered up the poison and gave the meat it's deceptively good taste."

The astronauts on the International Space Station saw something very peculiar as they were carrying out some repair jobs on the outside of their space station. At first they thought they were hallucinating, but then they discovered that all three could not be hallucinating exactly the same thing at exactly the same time. What they saw was a man covered in a cloud of what seemed to be hot spice and waving frantically for help. They also saw a number of cats, dogs, mice and rats, meowing, barking, squeaking and squalling. Like the man, they were surrounded by clouds of hot spice. The astronauts, using their jet propelled backpacks, flew over to the man and the beasts and hauled them into the space station where the man related what had happened at the Dimrun Hotel. NASA was informed of the bizarre phenomenon and the astronauts were ordered to return to Earth with their passengers immediately. After a few weeks of scientific testing and analyses, it was finally determined that the super-hot spices had trapped the air in the dense spicy cloud and had not only enabled the customer and the animals to breathe but had protected them from the dangerous cosmic rays in outer space.

Back on Earth, Walkees, Skipman and Uriah Heep were all tried, found guilty and sentenced. Heep was given 15 years and Skipman got 20 years. Nelson Dateland Walkees however was handed down a sentence of 35 years.

Dateland Walkees was feeling particularly sorry for himself one day. He entered the prison canteen one lunch-time and helped himself to the standard prison fare. When he had finished, one of the canteen ladies asked if he would like some more. As Walkees was feeling particularly hungry, he took up the offer. The lady took away his plate and returned with it loaded up with meat, potatoes and vegetables. After he had finished the meal, he began to feel somewhat peculiar. He thought he might be sick so he rushed out of the canteen and onto the prison's parade ground. His face started to go red and there developed a burning sensation in his mouth.

"Did you enjoy the meal?" asked a familiar voice from behind him. Walkees wheeled round and came face to face with Dermot Pans. "Since the Dimrun closed its doors, I've been looking around for alternative employment. So I landed this job as chef at the Krowbar Prison. Now before you blast off into orbit Walkees, let me remind you of a few things. You wanted me to be executed because I never really executed anything. Well, you've executed a lot of innocent people and all the things you ever executed in the Dimrun Hotel were theft and embezzlement. You were never an executive. All the executive decisions were taken by the Board – as a manager you just carried out orders. So, now Walkees, you have to become 'the executed manager'."

Walkees was trying to keep his mouth down – something he had never really been good at doing. He was literally attempting that feat this time. He passionately muttered and mumbled some protest through his nose.

"Oh don't complain Walkees, after all it's your philosophy old man, not mine".

Smoke was now coming out of Walkees' nose; it was coming out of his ears; it was coming out of his arse. He could no longer bear it; he opened his mouth and let out an almighty yell. Before he blasted off into space, Pans thrust a small radio into one of his hands.

Ten minutes later, Walkees radio started beeping. "Oh please, please get me down."

"Are you enjoying the view Walkees?" asked Pans.

"Are you just going to leave me to die up here? Soon the air in this spice cloud will become exhausted and I'll die of suffocation".

"You won't die of suffocation", Pans assured the poor wretch through the radio.

"Oh really? Oh thank goodness for that".

"Do you see the ISS nearby?"

"Yes, I see it."

"Swim-float over to it and get yourself in through the hatch. You see, the astronauts have been conducting some medical experiments lately. If you're lucky, they may have an anti-dote for salmonella poisoning".

What about Arup Kumar Singh Deo? You may be wondering what became of him. Did he manage to find a job? Indeed he did. At an Indian restaurant? No, at NASA's Jet Propulsion Laboratories in California!

And what about Michael Dimrun and his Board? They had to sell the hotel at a knock-down price. Where are they now? Oh they're still around. They can be seen at the Dimrun Hotel, now renamed The Wellrun Hotel. Michael Dimrun is the Head Waiter and the other members of the board all have jobs as either waiters or domestics. Who are the new owners? Often you can see a couple of Rolls Royces parked outside the hotel, and just as often you can see emerging from them the man in the pin striped suit and the man in the dicky bow tie.

Get Rich Quick.

I.

Charlie Chowkins and Jimmy Cowkins had been digging up London's streets for a long time. Charlie Chowkins had been engaged in this employment for 20 years and Jimmy Cowkins for 35 years. Charlie Chowkins in his early forties and Jimmy Cowkins in his mid-fifties didn't feel that life had exactly dealt them out a fair hand. When they laid their shovels and pneumatic drills aside to take their tea break around the brazier, their subject of conversation quite often centred around the concept of how they were getting older but not any richer.

"Still buying lottery tickets 'en Charlie?"

"Yeah, I'm still trying 'em Jimmy, but never any luck".

"Yi know, Charlie boy, they reckons that folks only 'as a one in a million chance of winning anyfing on 'i lottery."

"Right 'en Jim, but if ya never tries 'em, then for sure you'll never wins nofing. Ow's about you 'en Jim, are you still doin' the football pools?"

"Oh yeah, I'm still at it, but like you Charlie, I never wins nofing".

"So why do you keep on doin' em 'en Jimmy?"

"Same reason you does yer lottery tickets – I hopes to win one of 'em days".

"Say 'en Jim, wot would yer do if you won a pile of money?"

"I dunno, but I knows one fing Charlie, I wouldn't be diggin'up no more streets. Wot about you?"

"Same fing mate. I don't dig up streets 'cus it's me 'obby".

"Oh well, cheers 'en mate", said Jimmy Cowkins as they knocked their tin tea cups together.

"Yeah, cheers Jim", said Charlie Chowkins returning the toast.

As they were about to return to work, the door of one of the nearby houses opened and out came a lady dressed up to the nines in furs and jewellery. Over the years, Chowkins and Cowkins had dug up many streets in London. They had dug up streets in poor neighbourhoods and they had dug up streets in rich neighbourhoods. Presently they were digging up in a street near Barclay Square. When their work took them to the areas where the 'nobs' and 'toffs' lived, Chowkins and Cowkins often fantasised about "wot it would be likes to live in one of 'em 'ouses".

"All right for some, 'init?" said Jimmy Cowkins to Charlie Chowkins as they watched the lady walk down the garden path and out onto the street.

"Say Jim, 'o's she 'en"?

"Oh 'er. She's Mrs. Ruby Giltsilver. 'usband's a merchant of some kind or other".

"How comes yi know so much abou' 'em 'en Jim?"

"Oh Charlie me lad, I've been diggin' up London's streets longer 'an you 'ave, so I've sort a got to know one or two of 'em toffs", replied Jimmy Cowkins tapping the side of his nose with his right index finger.

Charlie Chowkins was only half listening to what his work-mate was saying. He just kept staring at Mrs. Giltsilver.

"You fancy 'er or somefing?" asked Jimmy.

"I fancy that necklace she's wearing. I'll betcha it's worth a bob or two".

"It's worth two million quid it is."

"Now 'ow do ya know that Jimmy me old mate? 'Ow cans ya possibly be so sure?"

"One day I was diggin' up a street near a jewellery shop in Knightsbridge. An' oo shoulds go into the shop but none other than Mr. & Mrs. Giltsilver. Charlie me boy, I was 'avin' me tea break at the time an' I heards everyfing – everyfing. I heards ém buyin' that necklace. Nofing escapes ol' Jimmy Cowkins, 'specially durin' 'is tea breaks. I tells ya Charlie lad, that necklace is worth two million smackers."

Charlie Chowkins simultaneously wiped his brow with the back of his hand and let out a whistle of astonishment.

"But 'ow does ya know it's the same necklace she's wearin' now?" Charlie wondered.

"Yer 'ol pal Jimmy Cowkins forgets neither a face nor a necklace".

II.

"Still thinkin' 'bout that necklace Charlie?" Jimmy Cowkins asked Charlie Chowkins. Cowkins had noticed the deeply reflective mood of his work-mate as the latter poured out their tea into the tin cups.

"If Mrs. Giltsilver there were to lose that necklace, would she be in dire poverty? I means, well, eh, I take it that all 'er money ain't in that necklace."

"Cor blyme no mate. 'Er an' 'er 'usband's so bleedin' rich that the loss of that necklace would be likes a mere drop in the ocean. I suppose 'twould be like you and me Charlie losing the price of a pint a beer. In fact, it's probably hinsured against loss and theft."

"Right 'en Jimmy. An' you an' me can't get hinsurance for our spilt beers now can we?"

"Never mind Charlie, money ain't everytfing. Ya know, ya can't take it wif ya when ya go."

Charlie agreed and after telling Jimmy that while there were indeed no pockets in a shroud, he could enjoy life as long as he was alive – and, of course – as long as he had the money with which the enjoyment could be purchased. Once more Charlie sunk into a reflective mood.

"You've got somefing on your mind, 'aven't you Charlie? Come on, out wif it, you can tell yer ol'pal Jimmy Cowkins about it".

"You say, Jimmy me ol'mucker, that the loss of that necklace would 'ardly make a dent in Mrs. Giltsilver's finances."

"Yeah".

"But it would make a hell of a difference to mine. So if I nicks 'er necklace, I gain but she doesn't loses".

"Now I takes it, Charlie, that you're talkin' 'ypothe'ical an'not hactual?"

"No Jimmy", said Charlie in low and serious tones, "I'm really finkin' of nickin' it".

"Ger ur of it", exclaimed Jimmy. "You surely ain't really".

"I am very, very serious. You wanna join me?"

"No way, Charlie. Sorry mate, but yer on yer own in this 'un".

"Now ya won't tell the bobbies on me now will ya?"

"My lips are sealed – I know nufing. But I ain't gonna be part of it."

"All right 'en Jimmy. You're me mate an' I just wanted to split it 50/50 wif ya".

"Cheers anywy mate, but I finks I'll be givin' 'is one a miss. Anyway, 'ow does ya plans to grab 'old a that necklace?"

"I've noticed that the necklace is clipped together at the back. So 'en, 'ere's wot I does. I runs up be'ind 'er undoes 'er necklace and I runs off as fast as me feet can carry me".

"She'll know oo yer ar. We've been diggin' up this 'ere street for more 'an a month now."

"I'll comes on Saturday wif a false beard an different clothes."

"All I can say is 'good luck 'en Charlie. But I'm 'avin'none of it."

"You always were the honest injun, Jim me old mate. Per'aps just that bit too honest for yer own good."

"Yi know wot they says about honesty bein' the best policy, Charlie?"

"I knows all about it Jimmy me old mucker. But ol'Charlie 'ere is gonna prove 'em all wrong."

"Six days to go 'en Charlie".

"In six days time, ol' Charlie's gonna be wuf two million quid".

III.

On the following Monday during their tea break Jimmy Cowkins smiled at his friend pityingly and said – 'ave yer done the awful deed 'en Charlie?"

"You bet I 'ave", replied his friend.

"In your dreams Charlie, in your dreams me old pal."

"I ain't kiddn ya Jimmy lad. I snatched that necklace clean off 'er neck".

"So why ain't you retirin' or off to the Ba'amas or sumfing?"

"Ye see Jimmy, if I don't turns up on the job 'ere then that would make it look suspicious. So, soon Jimmy me pal, soon. I'll takes it to a jeweller's shop and get me two million smackamaroos."

"Nice story Charlie boy, nice dream me ol' guvnor".

Charlie Chowkins raised his hand towards his cloth cap. "Are you ready for a shock Jimmy"? Chowkins removed his cap and there, lying on the top of his head was Mrs. Giltsilver's necklace!

"Bleed'n 'eck man!" screamed Cowkins. "But that's Mrs. Giltsilver's necklace."

"Of course it is; of course it is", said Chowkins slowly and calmly.

"But I fot you was only kidd'n."

"Then you fot wrong, didn't ya. Pretty necklace, init?"

Charlie placed the necklace back on the top of his head and covered it with his cloth cap.

"So when's you gonna take it to the jeweller's?" asked Jimmy Cowkins.

"Three or four days time I reckons. Now Jimmy, you ain't gonna blab are ya, you ain't gonna let the coppers know about this?"

"Don't you worry a fing, me ol' Charlie boy. Your secret is safe wif me".

On the following Saturday, Charlie walked into a very swanky jeweller's in London's West End and presented his stolen item for valuation.

"This is an exquisite piece of jewellery you have here", the jeweler commented when Charlie laid it on the counter. The

jeweler carefully examined it for about two or three minutes. "Mmmm, well, yes, it should fetch a very good price".

"How much exactly?"

"At a rough guess, mmm at today's prices – I would say between two to three million pounds".

"So are you interested in buying it from me?"

"Oh, absolutely. But first I must ascertain the exact value of the item. I shall now have to find out the current market prices for the various gem stones of which the necklace is composed. Would you excuse me one moment while I make a 'phone call?"

"Oh yeah, yeah of course."

"Do have a seat while I am 'phoning Mr. eh …"

"Chowkins is the name – Charlie Chowkins".

"I'll be back presently Mr. Chowkins".

Charlie Chowkins sat down and immediately went into a reverie about what he would do with all the money he was soon to acquire. He thought about Caribbean cruises and a chalet in Switzerland. He saw in his mind's eye a Rolls Royce purring to a halt outside the residence of Charles Chowkins Esq. He relished the thought of never having to work again. Dreams of a jet-setting lifestyle and dreams of champagne and caviar filled his imagination which was by now working overtime. Those sweet dreams were very rudely interrupted when the jeweler returned with a couple of police officers.

"Mr. Charles Chowkins?" asked one of the officers.

"Yes", answered an alarmed Charlie Chowkins.

"Mr. Chowkins", continued the officer, "is this necklace yours?"

"Yes – eh yes, it is". Poor Charlie was now shaking with fear.

"Could you please tell us where you obtained it?"

"Well, eh, yi see, eh this rich American aunt of mine died and eh left me it".

"Mr. Chowkins, would you please escort us to the police station?"

"Why? I 'aven't done nufing wrong".

"Mr. Chowkins", said the jeweler, "I am Lawrence Giltsilver the owner of this jewellery establishment. I recognise this necklace as the one that was stolen from my wife a week ago. I also recognise you as one of the labourers at the roadworks currently going on near our home."

IV.

Charlie Chowkins was charged, tried and convicted of violent assault and theft. He was given a five year prison sentence. At the end of his five year stretch, Charlie had to start his life all over again. He wondered if anyone would ever hire him again. Certainly, he could never go back to his old job on the roads.

There was something else that he wondered about too, and that was as to where his erstwhile chum and workmate might be. He had never come to visit him in prison, he had never even sent a Christmas card. In some ways Charlie felt let down by Jimmy. On closer reflection, he considered that he might just have wanted to protect himself. While he was never an accomplice to Charlie's wicked deed, he had known of Charlie's intention prior to the crime.

One day, he decided to go to Jimmy's house. When he got there, he found that Jimmy no longer lived there.

"Do you know where he went?" he asked the new occupants.

"The Cowkins moved out of here three years ago, but we have no idea as to where they went".

So, it seemed that Jimmy and Mavis had just disappeared. Maybe Jimmy had been laid off; maybe he found another job, or just simply retired. After further such speculation, Charlie became resigned to the loss of the only real friend that he had ever really had.

One evening after a day of fruitless searching for jobs, Charlie's 'phone started ringing. He wearily shuffled over to answer it.

"Is that Mr. Charlie Chowins?" asked the voice on the other end.

"Who is this?" asked Charlie in response.

"You remember me, me 'ol mucker?" answered the voice.

"Jimmy, is that you? Where are ya me ol' pal?"

"I'm in Bermuda."

"In Bermuda!! You 'avin'an 'oliday 'en?"

"Oh yeah, Charlie me ol' mate. I'm 'avin' an 'oliday all right. A permanent one. I lives 'ere now".

"Eh, you wot! How come? Did you get lucky on the lottery or the footie pools?"

"No none of that mate. I'll tell ya everyfing when you comes over".

"Come over?! You must be joking. I'm out of work and on the dole. I can barely afford a tube fare let alone an air ticket to Bermuda."

"I've paid your fare. There are two first class tickets for you and Doris. Just collect them from your nearest travel agency. You and Doris come over 'ere for a couple of weeks 'oliday."

Jimmy and Mavis Cowkins collected Charlie and Doris Chowkins from the airport in their state-of-the- art Bentley.

Their villa, with its manicured lawn and luxury swimming pool was a wonder to behold.

"Yi see Charlie", began Jimmy, as the two men were sitting in the bar of an expensive club, "I was really no more honest than you were. I was just that bit more subtle about it all."

"Blyme Guv, but 'ow did ya do it?"

"'ere's 'ow it all 'appened. All the years I was working on the roadworks, I got to know the neighbourhoods very well. I also got to know a lot about the people livin' in 'em. I eavesdropped on conversations near jeweller's shops and other expensive outfits. So I got to know oo was rich an' oo was poor. I noted down their names and addresses and after work was over I stayed behind in the ditches and dug tunnels under their houses. I would make man-holes with covers on their living-room floors and sneak in at night and start pilfering. I never took everything. I would never rob 'em blind. Usually just a few stones from bracelets, bangles and necklaces 'ere an'there. They'd never notice nofing. I kept a plan of all the tunnels I made so that when we dug up the roads again, I could complete unfinished tunnels from the last time or use finished ones to do a bit more nickin. Over the past 30 or so years I took all the valuables I nicked and sold 'em abroad durin' me 'olidays. I then salted the proceeds away in Swiss bank accounts."

"Wow, you're a genius".

"Now, wanna see sumthin?" Jimmy Cowkins slowly took off the sun-hat he was wearing. Charlie Chowkins' jaw dropped at what he saw. Sitting on top of Jimmy Cowkin's head was nothing other than Mrs. Giltsilver's necklace.

"Just before I retired I decided to do the bigee."

"You 'ad a tunnel leading to Mrs. Giltsilver's 'ouse?"

"Oh yeah. I've been robbin' that 'ouse for years. Mrs. Giltsilver and previous owners".

"Now wif you in jail, they couldn't blame you. And as there was no assault on Mrs. Giltsilver this time, and no signs of breaking and entry, she couldn't see how she could 'ave been robbed of it. I guess she musta come to the conclusion that she lost it. To be on the safe side, I'm going to sell it around the world".

"Just 'ow can ya do that?"

"I'll sell it in separate pieces in various markets in different countries. No-one will be any the wiser."

"Jee, you're a genius Jimmy".

"Never underestimate a cockney. An' never underestimate yer ol' Jim. Now listen 'en Charlie, yer ol' Jim's got a plan about 'ow you can bleed the ol' Giltsilvers dry".

V.

Providence had for Jeremy Chowkins, the son of Charlie and Doris Chowkins, mapped out quite a different path in life to that of his father. Jimmy Cowkins, in his greatly transformed financial situation, did not forget his old chum Charlie Chowkins. So, in his outstanding munificence, Mr. Cowkins paid for young Jeremy Chowkins' university education. Master Chowkins had shown a great keenness and bent for Philosophy – the only question was, what can you really do with it? After the graduation ceremony, at the University of Brixton, and after all the hand-shaking and congratulations, the real world had to be faced, and young Chowkins had to think about such things as a job, mortgage, school fees for future kids, car – well, you might say all the things needed to cope with life.

"You may 'ave a First in Philosophy", said Charlie to his son one day, "but you still 'as to pay the bills".

"You see Father, it is somewhat in the kidney of Mr. Micawber, something is bound to turn up one of these glorious days".

Part of Jimmy Cowkins' generosity had included elocution lessons for Chowkins junior, so as his father often said "my boy 'as learned 'ow to speak propah".

"All right Jerry me lad, you've got this laddy da heducation, but ya can't do nufing wif it. You may 'ave this philosophy stuff, bu' I prefers the opposite - reality".

"Well, Father, whilst it may not train one in the direction of any specific career or impart to one a particular skill, Philosophy, like so many of the subjects categorised under 'arts and humanities', does enable one to think in a style that is at once logical and critical, and thus, this form of reasoning may be transferred to many areas of human operation and endeavour."

"Eh – whazat you say?" responded a bewildered Charlie. Charlie often told Jeremy to speak English! The problem was that Jeremy often told his father to do the same.

"Anycase, 'ow's ya gettin' on wif Samantha Giltsilver? She's not gonna be hinterested in you."

"I shall be seeing her this afternoon, we're playing tennis at the club. She knows who I am and she knows who you are Father. You see, she has said to me on more than one occasion that she does not believe in the transference of the sins of the fathers to the sons. Her attitude is very much in the way of let bygones be bygones."

"So when do plans proposing to 'er?"

"Ho hum, well, that is still somewhat premature. I think that the courtship period must last a little longer, in fact, I think it should be extended into the new year."

"She ain't gonna marry you mate", said Chowkins senior. "You ain't got the background. The Giltsilvers an' them, they marries the likes o' the Rockefellers an' the Carnegies."

VI.

"I can 'ardly believe wot you is saying Jerry boy. This just can't be true".

"Well it is perfectly true Father. I shall soon be taking her round to introduce her to you and Mother."

"Well, it don't matter wot class she is or wot class we is, it's character wot matters", said Doris Chowkins. "I finks it's wonderful that the Giltsilvers an' the Chowkins are going to be united."

"Just sumfing you should consider Jerry: she's rich an' you're poor. You're gonna be under 'er thumb", Charlie said.

"Not at all. Samantha and I have already had a heart to heart talk on this very issue. I have made it clear to her that I don't want any of this women's lib stuff. I am the boss and that is that."

"I'll bet she's blown you out already", sneered Charlie.

"This is where you are quite wrong Father. She has agreed to this. She will not use her money to dominate me."

"All right 'en. We'll see 'ow it all pans out".

Jeremy and Samantha were married in a magnificent ceremony in a magnificent church and there followed a magnificent wedding dinner. Jeremy and Samantha Chowkins then embarked upon a magnificent honeymoon on a magnificent cruise in the south Pacific.

Having married into money, Jeremy wanted for nothing. He just asked Samantha and Samantha gave him money. He wore the most expensive of clothes, drove a top of the range car and went on the most luxurious holidays. They lived in a huge three storey mansion in Queen Anne Street near Barclay Square and, when they wanted to just get away from it all, they went to either their country estate in the Cotswolds, their villa in Switzerland or their chalet in the south of France.

Indeed, money was no object, yet in spite of all this, this, which most people cannot even dream of, Jeremy was not a totally happy man. There was just one thing that kept niggling at him. He had never managed to pluck up the courage to speak to Samantha about it; instead he just kept putting it off, hoping that he would get used to it. Yet, not only did he not get used to it, it actually grew like a cancer and tormented the life out of him. More and more did he become annoyed by it. After a year of marriage, it was keeping him awake at night, he was obsessed by it during the day, he ate and drank it with every meal – it was always at the front of his thoughts. Even sleep did not keep this monster at bay, for he dreamt about it in the very dead of the night. At last, he could bear it no longer – he would have it out with Samantha.

"Samantha, you have been refusing a lot of my requests for money lately. Like yesterday, when I asked you for a hundred thousand pounds to install some devices in my Jaguar."

"Jerry dear, we are going through difficult economic times at the moment. We have to draw in the reins a bit".

"But Samantha darling, I find it rather humiliating to have to continuously ask you for money for everything I want."

"I have given you the money most of the times you have asked."

"Most of the time, but not all of the time".

"Jerry, you are forgetting that you do not have money of your own. You came into this marriage poor, I came in rich".

"Now Samantha, you are really spelling it out, you are truly rubbing it in. We are married, we are one, what is yours is mine and what is mine is yours".

"But that's just it Jerry, you have nothing".

"There you go again, rubbing it in."

"I'm not rubbing anything in Jerry, I'm just telling the truth. And anyway, you brought up the subject, not I".

"This subject is long overdue for analysis and overhaul, Samantha".

"What exactly do you mean Jerry? Just what exactly are you getting at?"

"You are the one that has just pointed out my penurious situation at the time of our marital union. I think that this ought to be rectified."

"And exactly how do you think it should be rectified Jerry dear?"

"I want you to put all your financial resources into my name".

VII.

"You must be absolutely mad Jerry, absolutely mad. You've taken complete leave of your senses", screamed Samantha.

"No I haven't", retorted Jeremy. "You agreed prior to our marriage that I am the boss and that I would have none of this women's liberation nonsense."

"Indeed I did. But that does not require me to hand over all my assets to you. The law does not require me to do this. Really Jerry, this is 2010, not 1810!"

"A married woman should have no property. She ought to be stripped of her assets and that these be brought under her husband's control".

Samantha Chowkins looked at her husband in utter disbelief. "Jerry", she began, "whatever your personal views on this subject may be, you cannot force me to hand over my financial resources to you. You are completely off your rocker. In 1875, Parliament passed a law which allowed married women to own property and have other assets in their own name and apart from their husbands."

"I'm not talking about the law Samantha, I'm talking about you and me."

"Jerry darling, while I don't believe in women's lib, I don't believe in women's enslavement either. But I do believe in women's rights."

"You have no rights Samantha".

"That is absolutely outrageous. As a Philosophy graduate you should know that what you are saying is completely illogical".

"As a Philosophy graduate, I can tell you that there is neither logic nor illogic in saying that men or women have or haven't rights. This is all a matter of personal opinion and value judgement".

"Oh well then Jerry, your value judgement and my value judgement are equal, but there is a law which clearly states that women can have property under their own name."

"Samantha? Can we play a little game? Forget value judgements and forget personal opinions – forget even the law. I can show you by a process of logical argument that I have a water-tight case for asking you, nay, demanding from you, your entire assets."

"Well, that's impossible", snapped an angry Samantha.

"If you are so sure then Samantha sweetheart why don't you play my game?"

"And what precisely is this game that you want me to play?" replied Samantha haughtily throwing her head back.

"It is this. If I can show you by solid logic that I am entitled to your assets, and you fail to produce a counter logic to my argument, then you hand over your assets to me."

"All right. I'll play your game. I feel perfectly confident in winning for you have no legal or moral case to ask for my assets".

"Good", said Jeremy Chowkins quietly, "then let the game begin".

"Hummmph".

"Now Samantha – first question: when you married me, did you want to marry a man or a woman?"

Samantha threw back her head in contemptuous laughter. "Good heavens, Jeremy. Is that the best you can come up with?"

Jeremy merely looked her cold in the eye and repeated the question.

"Well, of course I wanted to marry a man. I'm not a lesbian."

"Second question", continued Jeremy. "When I married you, did I want to marry a man or a woman?"

"Well, Jeremy dearest, unless you have kept something back from me concerning your past, I'm convinced your desire was for a woman. Unless I'm terribly mistaken, you are not a homosexual".

By now Samantha was in a fit of giggles, but Jeremy, unperturbed, continued as coldly and calmly with his questioning.

"Now dear, do you consider me as a man or a woman?"

"Well of course I consider you as a man – I would never have married you otherwise".

"And do you consider yourself as a woman?"

"Yes of course. I am all woman", said Samantha through her giggles. "You know Jerry, I thought you were an intelligent guy – something of a Plato or an Aristotle."

"Now Samantha. We are agreed so far. Right?"

"Right", laughed his wife.

"But you are not allowing me to function as a man. By having me coming to ask, nay, beg you for money, you are detracting from my manhood".

At once the giggles stopped. "Well, eh well…."

"Well, can you give a reasoned argument in denial of that?"

"Eh, well…eh…I must admit you've got me there".

"Good, we're still in agreement, right?"

"Well, eh yes, so far though".

"Now, let's continue", said Jeremy in victorious tones, "by your holding the money and having the final say on its use, you are acting more like the husband than the wife. Can you deny this?"

Samantha was now struggling to find an answer. Her giggling had now completely stopped. She appeared at once both thoughtful and chastened.

"No, this would appear to be right".

"It most definitely is – whoever controls the money controls all. Correct?"

"Well, eh, yes, eh correct".

"As things stand in this household Samantha, you are playing the masculine role and I am playing the feminine role".

"It would seem to be so".

"In this case you are contradicting your original statements that you wanted to marry a man and I wanted to marry a woman. You further contradict your own claims to womanhood and mine to manhood."

Samantha could simply not answer. She could think of no logical argument with which to counter her husband's ruthless reasoning.

"You have won a few battles but not the war", cried Samantha in a highly defensive manner. But it was now clear that she was very much on the defensive.

"Let us continue."

"I don't wish to continue this silly nonsense any further", said Samantha sulkily.

"If you stop now my dear, you will have lost. It is in your best interests to continue. And you did say at the beginning of all this that you could easily demolish my arguments."

"Perhaps I still can".

"Okay then. Let us waste no further time. Let us in fact, in our mind's eye go back to the time of our wedding. Did not one of the marriage vows I had to take proceed somewhat like 'with all my worldly goods I thee endow'?"

"But Jeremy sweetest, you had no worldly goods with which to endow me."

"Aha!" exclaimed Jeremy triumphantly, "precisely".

"So?"

"So – in order for me to faithfully fulfill my marriage vow, it is necessary for you to transfer all your worldly goods to me. Then, Samantha sweetie, I can start doing the endowing, eh?"

"But but…."

"And in order to reverse the currently topsy turvy situation where husband is wife and wife is husband, your money must be transferred into my name?"

"I…..I…"

"You, you agree with me", said her husband scornfully. "At least you agree with me implicitly in that you cannot find any counter-argument".

"This is most unfair", retorted Samantha.

"Unfair?" asked her husband mockingly, "unfair? You agreed to play my game of logic, so don't say that I am unfair. You were convinced you would win and yet you have not been able to come up with even one opposing argument. Now Samantha – here is my trump card. My four vows were to love, honour, cherish and protect. Look at the last of these – protect. I am charged with the responsibility of not only protecting your person but protecting your property, and surely the best way of protecting it is when it is in my name and my possession. As long as your property is in your name, my hands are tied in terms of protecting it. Agreed?"

Samantha remained silent. She thought hard but could come up with no answer.

"You're not doing too well are you my dear? Now – repeat to me your four marriage vows, Samantha."

"To love, honour, cherish and obey".

"What was the last of those four Samantha love?"

"Obey".

"So by refusing to sign over your assets to me, you are breaking one of your marriage vows".

"Other women do not hand over their properties to their husbands when they opt to obey them in the marriage ceremony. And the law does not see it that way."

"I am not talking about other women or about what the law sees. Remember Samantha, this game is between you and me only. Now when you said 'obey' you wrote me a blank cheque. Didn't you realise that? There was no qualification at all put on that verb. Not 'obey in some things', or 'obey in most things' or 'obey in what I choose to obey in', you simply said 'obey'.

By now, Samantha was devastated, she kept staring blankly at the window behind her husband.

"Tell me Samantha", her husband went on, "do you like the idea of being someone who does not stick to agreements, someone who even breaks solemn vows? Is that the sort of person you are? Is that the sort of reputation you want to have?"

"Well – n n n no, no of course not", Samantha blurted out.

"Excellent", said her husband in the ascending tone of one triumphant, "we are in perfect harmony. You and I Samantha are on exactly the same wave-length".

"I just want to be the perfect wife", whimpered Samantha.

"Oh you are going to be Samantha, you are going to be", replied Jeremy with a cunning edge to his voice. "Now – another question. What ceremony did your father perform during the wedding service?"

"He gave me away."

"And to whom were you given, Samantha?"

"I was given to you Jeremy."

"Exactly. Now, if you were given to me, then all your property was likewise given to me. You see Samantha, it is logically and rationally impossible for your property to be anyone else's but mine. When you were given to me, logic and reason gave your property to me. You cannot say your property is yours for the simple reason that you were given to me. When you were given to me, I became your owner, so your property is like you, it is, by sheer reason, in my possession".

For a full five minutes, there reigned a total silence in the living-room. It was Jeremy who broke the silence. "Samantha, next week, we are going to the lawyers to transfer all your property into my name."

"No", replied Samantha firmly.

"No?" said her husband indignantly.

"No", replied Samantha again and just as firmly as before. "We are going to make the transfer tomorrow".

"You know", said her husband holding her and gently caressing her, "I love you very much. But you must understand that I am the authority. You must be obedient and submissive. Samantha, you are a real woman now".

"And Jeremy, you are a real man".

"The right order of things has been restored in this marriage".

"What exactly shall I possess Jeremy dear?"

"Not a penny. You will live like a queen, but I shall control the money."

VIII.

Five years later, the marriage between Charlie and Samantha Chowkins was on the rocks.

"I'm really getting tired of all the wrong investment and business decisions you make", yelled Samantha during one of their fights.

"And I'm sick of you stepping out of line. Your job is to feed babies and keep nice house. It is not your prerogative to criticise the decisions of your husband."

Samantha simply sat on the sofa with folded arms.

"And another thing, Mrs. Chowkins, I am not tolerating any more of this sulkiness. I expect better of you. Now go and make some tea."

Up got Samantha and obediently but unwillingly went to the kitchen. She returned and laid the tea tray on the small table near her husband. The two drank their tea in silence. Not a word was said between them.

"Now clear these things away and then come back, there is something I wish to talk about".

Angrily and huffily Samantha took the tray through to the kitchen. She washed the dishes and then returned to her husband who was waiting in the living-room.

"Now Samantha, I am filing for divorce."

"Oh really?" was all Samantha's reply.

"You don't look too surprised".

"Who is she?"

"Better than you".

"A woman of property and means no doubt."

"Benjamin Disraeli once said that it is as easy to marry a rich woman as it is to marry a poor one. So I go for the rich ones."

"So you only married me for my money?"

"No, for your beauty, your intelligence and for your obedience also."

"But money was part of it?"

"Of course. I have a right to expect you to bring something into the marriage".

Samantha threw back her head huffily.

A decree nisi was soon attained and Mr.& Mrs. Chowkins were divorced.

"Pack your bags madam", commanded Jeremy, "and leave this house".

"Now that we are divorced, this house reverts to me".

"Neither according to the law nor the little game we agreed to. And you are the one who kept invoking the law if you remember. Well, the law says everything is split down the middle. You have no assets though to be split".

"In that case I am entitled to half of your assets".

"Not according to our little game. And we're still playing it".

"Explain".

"Well, first of all you are still Mrs. Jeremy Chowkins, married or divorced, that is your name. Secondly, when you agreed to obey me, you wrote a blank cheque – remember?"

"Yes, I remember. But that is only so long as we remain married".

"Wrong again. What did we say? It was 'til death us do part', not 'til divorce us do part'. You are therefore still under a solemn and binding obligation to be dutiful and obedient towards me".

"I uh eh… well…but that's only looking at it from a logician's point of view".

"And what, pray tell me madam is more logical than logic? And did we not agree that this game is based on logic?"

"Ye e e es", stammered Samantha.

"Very well madam, you walk out of this house destitute".

Samantha Chowkins managed to find lodgings in a run-down part of Stockwell in London. She found a humble job as a secretary but due to her skills and business acumen she rose in the company, first to a managerial position and then to a directorship. Contrariwise, Jeremy Chowkins' fortunes started to sink. Bad investment decisions ensured that he lost all of the money he had obtained from his first marriage and it was not long before he squandered all the money he obtained from his second marriage. Yet, Jeremy Chowkins had a plan up his sleeve.

One evening, while she was sitting in her mews flat in Mayfair, Samantha Chowkins heard a ring on her doorbell. She got up from her comfortable sofa and went to see who it could be.

"Good evening Mrs. Chowkins", said Jeremy Chowkins rather haughtily as he stood on Samantha's doorstep.

"What do you want here? I don't want to have anything more to do with you".

"Ah but I want to have something to do with you Mademoiselle", said Jeremy arrogantly as he invited himself into the flat.

"This is trespass. I don't recall inviting you in".

"I don't need your invitation madam. And it is not trespass as according to the rules of our game I am perfectly entitled to come in here. Don't forget, you are still subject to my authority."

"What exactly do you want?"

"First of all, a glass of champagne madam". Samantha obediently poured her ex-husband some champagne.

"And secondly?"

"I understand you are doing rather well in the company you are currently working for".

"Yes. So?"

"So Madam, tell me what your income is". At once Samantha showed him her salary and other entitlements from the company. "Good now. I want 20% of that."

"But… but…"

"There are no 'buts' about it. You promised to obey me unconditionally. Now agree to this 20% before I raise it to 30% or even higher."

"I am an honourable woman and because of the rules of the game, a game I agreed to, I shall give you the 20% to which you are entitled."

Jeremy Chowkins simply had no head for business. He soon managed to lose most of what was left of his former wife's and second wife's assets. All that was left was the house in Queen Anne Street near Barclay Square. The income he received from his ex's earnings didn't stretch too far. He realised that sooner or later he would have to get a job.

One morning the post-man delivered a very strange letter. It was an invitation from the editor of a newly launched newspaper asking interested parties to come for interviews for the position of investigative reporter. Jeremy Chowkins at once started fantasising about being a top notch, first class investigative reporter. He told his wife that he "was going to go for it".

"Good luck with it, my dear", said Mrs. Chowkins the Second as Jeremy left home in his best suit for the job interview.

"All right then, Mr. Chowkins", said Robert Clout, the editor of *The London Daily*. "I think you could do the job. Now when can you start?"

"As soon as possible, Mr. Clout", answered Jeremy enthusiastically.

"Can you start next Monday?"

"Yes of course".

"Good show, Mr. Chowkins, good show", said Clouts rising and warmly shaking Chowkins by the hand.

IX.

"Welcome aboard Mr. Chowkins", said Robert Clout the following Monday morning. "I want to start you off on a fairly tough assignment. Now I know this is a bit of being, well like, thrown in at the deep end, but if you think it's too difficult just tell me. I'll understand perfectly if you wish to decline".

"Oh no, Mr. Clout, I can rise to the challenge I'm sure. I mean, I'll certainly have a stab at it, I'll do my very best".

"That's the spirit, Jeremy, that's the spirit. I like a man who doesn't shrink from a challenge."

"And may I ask what exactly it is you would like me to investigate?"

"There's this company called DNA Manipulation Enterprises. Their chief scientist, a Professor Bertie Barnistry, is supposedly conducting some highly controversial research."

"And what exactly is the nature of this research?"

"Well Jeremy, if we knew that we wouldn't need to investigate".

"Have you tried interviewing Professor Barnistry before?"

"Yes, on a couple of occasions, but he declined. His staff at the company's laboratories have been sworn to secrecy, so we can't get anything out of them either".

"So why do you think that I might succeed where other more experienced journalists have failed?"

"We don't know until we try. You seem to have the right attitude Jeremy. You are motivated by ambition and drive."

"You know Mr. Clout, I think I may be able to succeed where other reporters have failed".

"Really now Jeremy? And why is that?"

"Well, my ex wife is a director of that very company."

"Wow!" exclaimed Clout, "you don't say."

"Yes, indeed she is".

"But why will she break silence? Even if she were still married to you, she would remain under an obligation of loyalty to the company to keep things hushed up".

"I am quite sure that I can persuade Samantha to tell us what we want to know about the research at DNA Manipulation Enterprises".

"Now Jeremy. I hope by that that you don't intend to use violence or some such thing on your ex. We want to keep this legit. and within the law. This newspaper is struggling to get a reputation in the community so we can't afford any expensive lawsuits."

"Believe me, Mr. Clout, I can obtain the information in a perfectly legal and legitimate manner."

As he confidently strode towards the door of Samantha's flat, Chowkins knew that all he had to do was to play the 'obey card'. He turned the handle of the door, but found it to be locked. He rang the bell, but there was still no answer. He knocked a number of times, but no-one came to open the door. Chowkins then got out his mobile phone and dialed Samantha's mobile number – but he had no luck. He tried her land line and her work number, but she remained incommunicado.

"So did you manage to get any info. from your ex wife?" Robert Clout asked Jeremy a couple of days later.

"I've been going to her flat and phoning all her numbers, but I just can't seem to make any contact."

"Did you try 'phoning the company itself?"

"Oh yes, but they were completely unhelpful. All I got were rather sniffy answers telling me that the whereabouts of their employees couldn't be given to unauthorised personnel."

"I just hope your ex is all right. Anyway, it seems that you'll have to go directly to Professor Barnistry's laboratories".

"Yes, there really is nothing else for it but that."

So off went Jeremy to the laboratories. At the reception desk he was curtly told that Professor Barnistry never gave interviews.

"Are you Professor Barnistry's secretary?" Chowkins asked the young blonde receptionist. Jeremy Chowkins was acting in a rather smarmy manner as he knew perfectly well that the girl was merely the receptionist and not in any way connected to the professor's office.

"No, Mr. Chowkins, I'm only the receptionist around here".

"Oh, that's a pity. I take it the professor must be a bit short-sighted".

"Really, Mr. Chowkins? Whatever would cause you to presume such a thing?"

"Well, that he would keep a beautiful woman like you at reception rather than in his office as his secretary?"

"Oh, Mr. Chowkins", said the young lady blushing, "I'll bet you say this sort of thing to all the girls".

"I do. But the only difference is that I mean it with you".

"Mr. Chowkins you really are the quintessential charmer".

"And stop calling me 'Mr. Chowkins', Jeremy's the name".

"All right then Jeremy", said the blonde giggling.

"Tell me pretty maid indeed, are there any more at home like you?" Jeremy sang out the first stanza of that old song as he put his arm around the young blonde's waist.

"Oh Jeremy, you must stop doing this", giggled the lass.

"You haven't told me your name yet?"

"It's Susan."

"What a lovely name. A lovely name for a lovely lady".

"Jeremy?"

"Yes?"

"Do you want to have that interview with Professor Barnistry?"

"Yes, but I'm rather enjoying this interview with you right now".

Susan took Jeremy's arm to the door and pointed to a large building about a couple of hundred yards away.

"Those are the laboratories", she whispered to Chowkins. "But I never showed them to you – right?"

"Right", Chowkins whispered back.

"The professor may or may not be there – but that's where to look".

"Good. Now, how about dinner with me somewhere this evening?"

"Jeremy! But you're a married man", exclaimed the girl.

"How would you know whether or not I'm a married man?" said Jeremy somewhat inquiringly and taking one step back from the receptionist.

"Oh, come on now. A handsome man like you - unmarried. I can't believe it".

"Well, no problem. What she never knows will never hurt her".

"I'll think about it Jeremy, but first, go and see if you can find the professor".

X.

Jeremy Chowkins marched enthusiastically towards the laboratories. He felt he had really triumphed with his charms – not only by gaining access to the laboratories but by maybe even getting a night out with the blonde.

As he walked into the building, his heart sank somewhat; he encountered another receptionist, this time though a fat 50 year old with multiple chins and a fiery expression on her face.

"I D please", she said in a grating voice.

Chowkins showed the battle-ax his press ID card. The battle-ax looked at it with an appalled expression on her face.

"Are you a research worker or a laboratory technician, Mr. Chowkins? Do you work here in the laboratory in any capacity?"

"Eh, well no".

"Well, I am afraid Mr. Chowkins that you are not authorised to enter these premises".

"But, eh, you see, Professor Barnistry is expecting me. We made an arrangement to meet at this time", lied Chowkins.

The battle-ax proceeded to look through a large appointment book. She was obviously Professor Barnistry's secretary. "I'm sorry Mr. Chowkins but there is no appointment recorded here."

"But surely there is some mistake then", persisted Chowkins, "I spoke to Professor Barnistry on the 'phone and we made an appointment for 11am".

"Please sit down Mr. Chowkins and I shall attempt to locate Professor Barnistry".

Jeremy Chowkins took a seat in the laboratory's reception area while the battle-ax left in search of her boss.

"Good God", thought Jeremy to himself, "imagine Barnistry choosing that thing as a secretary rather than the gorgeous blonde over at the main reception. He's either a raving faggot or is extremely loyal to his wife".

Ten minutes went by, then fifteen, then twenty minutes went by, but there was no sign of the battle-ax returning. After half an hour, Chowkins' patience was beginning to run out. He got up off his chair and started pacing up and down the reception room. Walking over to the door that connected the laboratory with the reception, Chowkins wondered if he should 'sneak a peek'. He looked at his watch and decided not to, so he started pacing again. Getting bored with the pacing, he began taking a closer look at the paintings which graced the walls of the reception. Then he studied the plants, the ornaments on the secretary's desk, the mosaics on the floor and the intricate patterning on the border where the walls and the ceiling met. With the conviction that he could get nothing more out of the 'culture' of the reception room which he had studied in the minutest of detail, he considered that it was either a case of sneaking that peek or leaving. He then decided that he would leave.

As he was about to exit, a man's voice called from within the laboratory – "Mr. Jeremy Chowkins, come in here please".

"Ah", thought Chowkins, "that must be Barnistry". He started to feel more hopeful.

Chowkins pushed open the laboratory door and stepped inside. The room was pitch dark and Chowkins could see nothing.

"Please turn on the light – the switch is on your left as you come in from the reception", said the mysterious voice which Chowkins presumed to be that of Professor Barnistry. Chowkins fumbled about near the door and eventually found the switch. When he flicked it, a few dim lights came on.

Chowkins squinted his eyes somewhat as he could still not see very much. Only about three rather weak lights lit up the cavernous room. Chowkins' breath was taken away by what he eventually saw: the laboratory was filled with shoulder high long narrow rectangular stands. On top of each stand was a human head. When Chowkins steadied himself, he came to the conclusion that they must simply be dummies.

"Welcome Mr. Chowkins", said the voice.

Chowkins looked to his right and to his absolute horror noticed that one of the heads was speaking.

"What is this? Some sort of ventriloquism?"

"Touch me", said the head.

Chowkins accepted the offer and shrunk back in terror when he realised that he had touched human flesh.

"Agghhhhh" shrieked Chowkins. " Bloody hell, what sort of a place is this? Who or – should I say, what are you?"

"My name is Peter Porter. I'm what you might call the Head head around here?"

"Is this some sort of joke?"

"Tell him lads and lasses", hollered out Peter Porter.

"We're all heads together here", yelled out about 20 heads in chorus.

Jeremy Chowkins heart was now pounding. He was beginning to wish he had never come to this place.

Peter Porter then invited Jeremy to open a large filing-cabinet type drawer at the far end of the room. Jeremy walked over to it but hesitated in front of it.

"Open it Jeremy", said another nearby head.

Jeremy opened the drawer and let out a cry.

"Hello Jeremy, nice to see you again. Still fancy going out with me tonight?"

Jeremy Chowkins slammed shut the drawer. It was the head of Susan the receptionist.

"Of course you could always go out with me", said another head on one of the pillar type structures.

Chowkins almost vomited when he descried the head of the battle-ax secretary. He rushed down the room again to where the Head head, Peter Porter was located.

"What the hell is going on here? What is all this about?" demanded Jeremy of Peter.

"You see, we are all patients who, when we had our bodies, were suffering from terminal illnesses. Now Professor Bertie Barnistry has devised a way of extending our lives. While we wait for the day when cures to our illnesses are found, our bodies are destroyed but our heads remain."

"Good God Almighty", said Jeremy with his hands firmly clasped on his cheeks. "But how are you kept alive. What about blood flow and nutrients and other such life support?"

"I'm just coming to that. Underneath the supports on which our heads rest are thousands of miniature organs cloned and grown from our DNA. They dangle from the base of our necks. Our legs, arms, hearts, kidneys and so forth are all there in miniature form. But instead of one or two of these there are thousands. So an adequate supply of blood is supplied to our brains. Our nutrients are supplied intravenously".

"But how does this stop the cancerous growths?"

"Every day, the professor and his staff grow new organs from our DNA and throw out the previous day's ones. This way the tumours are kept at bay".

"Don't you get bored just eh well eh sitting here permanently?"

"Not really. We get used to it. We can read, we can watch TV, we can listen to music. Part of the duties of the lab. staff is to bring us reading material which they place in front of us. It's all electronic stuff and we can turn pages simply by electrical impulses from our thought processes. We're all having a whale of a time here."

"Well, I'll be damned", said Chowkins, "I'll be damned", he repeated. "So this is what Professor Barnistry's up to. What a scoop this is going to be for my newspaper". Already Chowkins was dreaming of a career in Fleet Street and fantasised about being editor of *The Sunday Times*.

"So you're a newspaper man eh?"

"Yeah, yeah I am. And a real top one at that", boasted Chowkins.

All of a sudden, Chowkins was grabbed from behind. A chloroform soaked cloth was put over his nose and mouth. He was soon unconscious.

XI.

Jeremy Chowkins slowly started to come to. He thought all this had just been a bad dream and that he would wake up safe in his own bed next to his own dear wife. It was pitch dark again, the same darkness that he had experienced when he first entered the laboratory. Chowkins tried to move his limbs but found that to be impossible. As the affect of the chloroform started to wear off and he could therefore think and see more clearly, he realised that he had no sensation at all in his body. "This must be the effect of the drug I was given", he thought.

Someone, somewhere in the room switched on a light. Jeremy's eyes were beginning to focus more clearly. He struggled hard to move but could not. The same lack of sensation persisted. As his eyes became adjusted to the poor lighting conditions, he looked around and saw that he was in the laboratory. He rapidly opened and closed his eyes hoping that instead of the laboratory, the familiar surroundings of his own bedroom would come into clear and sharp focus. No matter how many times he blinked, the same scene of the laboratory presented itself to him. He understood now that it was no dream.

Chowkins tried hard to move his body but the sense of numbness persisted. His eyes were the only parts of his anatomy that allowed him any mobility. He looked up and saw the ceiling of the laboratory. He looked sideways and saw the heads. Then, on lowering his eyes he beheld a sight which made him want to flee in fear. The problem was that he had nothing which could provide the locomotion for flight. It now dawned on him – he was a head.

Chowkins' voice still seemed to be there. "Help, help, he shouted".

"Why are you shouting?" asked Peter Porter the Head head. "You are disturbing everyone. Be silent".

"Why have they done this to me?" sobbed Jeremy.

"Well I'm sure I don't know", answered Peter.

A few minutes later some strange things began to happen in the laboratory. The heads started regaining their limbs and other parts of their bodies. Legs, hands, arms, trunks all started to appear on the heads. Peter Porter's arms were dangling at the side of his support pillar. Very soon his legs appeared. There before Jeremy was the bizarre sights of Peter Porter with his arms and legs, but no trunk, waddling about on the laboratory floor. Before not too long, the laboratory floor was littered with heads having attached to them various parts of their hitherto missing anatomy. Some heads had trunks but no limbs. Others had limbs but no trunks. And some others would have one leg or one arm. About five minutes later all the heads had their bodies back. They popped back into existence like balloons being pumped full of air.

"This can't be real", reasoned Jeremy. "This can only be a nightmare I'm going through".

"Oh, we are real enough", said one of the former heads.

"You see", said Peter Porter, "the professor has not yet managed to perfect the technique, so sometimes the miniature organs all come together and develop into full-blown organs. So you may yet be able to get away".

All the 'heads' now started walking out of the laboratory. They all wished Jeremy good luck!

Jeremy Chowkins was now all alone. He could only resign himself to his fate and hope that either Barnistry or some of his assistants would come and rescue him from this awful situation.

Eventually, the door opened and in walked three men. One of them looked much older and Jeremy took this man to be Professor Bertie Barnistry.

"Well John, how are you now?" asked the older man.

"I'm not John", replied Chowkins.

"What? You are John Wilkins are you not?"

"My name is Jeremy Chowkins."

"Oh dear then, I think there has been some mistake. Why are you here?"

"I am a reporter from *The London Daily*. I came here to interview you".

"Did you indeed now?"

"I take it you are Professor Bertie Barnistry?"

"You have taken it right, my man", answered the professor rather harshly. "And what are you doing nosing around my laboratory?"

"You are illegally holding me here. This is called kidnapping Professor."

"And what you have been doing is called trespassing".

"Will you kindly return my body to me?"

"Yes of course. At first we thought you were a patient of ours, a certain Mr. John Wilkins. That's why you are in this condition."

"Then for God's sake get me out of this".

"It's not that easy, Mr. Chowkins. The law requires that before we can restore the body to a head, we must get the next of kin's consent. Who is your next of kin, Mr.Chowkins".

"Well, my father, Mr. Charles Chowkins is. But look, all these other heads obtained their bodies without intervention of next of kin".

"That happened by accident, Mr. Chowkins. That was due to flaws in the technique. However, you have been given a revised and perfected formula so there is less likelihood of you growing back your body naturally."

Chowkins gave Barnistry his wife's number but on trying it could find no-one at home.

He then gave Barnistry his parents' contact details. A few minutes later Barnistry returned and informed the unfortunate Chowkins that his parents had just flown off to Bermuda for a month's holiday with their friends the Cowkins.

"Is there no-one else?" Barnistry asked.

"Well, there is my ex wife, I suppose".

A few minutes later Barnistry returned but with the bad news that they could not make telephonic contact with her.

"Your ex wife is a director of this company, Mr. Chowkins".

"Yes I know and she will for sure sign whatever needs to be signed in order to get me out of this. Surely you must be able to contact her within the company's communications system".

"Yes for sure, that is the best course of action".

About ten minutes later, Barnistry and his two assistants returned with the news that they had finally made contact with Samantha Chowkins.

"Great!" sighed Jeremy with relief. "Will she be here soon?"

"She says she can't come", answered Barnistry.

"What, why not?"

"You see, she said something or other about a game that you two play. It started during your marriage and continues even after your divorce. She says that she can only obey you."

"Then tell her to obey me by coming here right away".

"The problem is that she says that her vow was to you and you alone. She cannot answer such a summons indirectly. Her argument is that she cannot be sure that I or my staff are telling the truth, so she finds it impossible according to the rules of your game to answer a command that has come from what may well be, in her mind at least, dubious sources."

"Then put her on the 'phone. Place your mobile next to my ear and I'll order her to come here".

"I suggested that to her, but she says she could never be sure that the voice is really yours. Given the weirdness of the situation that has been described to her, she could not be sure of the authenticity of your voice."

"As a director of this company, she must know about the experiments that go on here".

"Not this one. Only the Chairman, Vice Chairman and my two senior assistants, and of course the patients know about this."

"Then what can be done? You can't leave me like this forever."

"In order to ascertain the authenticity of all this, your wife has suggested that you sign your name on this piece of paper. We will deliver the signed paper to her and she will at once recognise your signature."

"How can I sign something without my hands and arms?" protested Chowkins.

"I can grow your arm for that purpose. Are you left or right handed Mr. Chowkins?"

"Right handed".

One of Barnistry's assistants started fiddling about with the side of the pillar on which Chowkins' head rested. Within a few minutes, Chowkins had his right arm and hand back. He signed the piece of paper.

An hour later, the three men came back into the room. "Well Mr. Chowkins I have good news and bad news for you."

"Tell me the bad news first".

"Eh, I'd prefer to begin with the good news which is that your wife has recognised your signature and has signed all the documents necessary for the re-growth of your body".

"That's great, just great. I don't need to know the bad news as nothing could be as bad as the nightmare I have just undergone".

XII.

Ten minutes later, Jeremy Chowkins had his body back. At first he was a bit unsteady on his feet, but eventually his blood circulation was fully restored and he was able to move quite freely. Professor Barnistry and the two assistants led Chowkins through the reception area and towards Barnistry's office.

"Sit down, please Mr. Chowkins", said Barnistry. "Tea or coffee?"

"Tea if you please".

Barnistry picked up his office intercom and ordered two cups of tea. About five minutes later a lady came into the office with a tray on which were the two cups of tea and a plateful of biscuits.

"I think it is now appropriate to inform you of the bad news, Mr. Chowkins", said Barnistry.

"Well, I'm not really interested", responded Chowkins rather contemptuously and dismissively. "After having lost my entire body and then having had it restored, I cannot think that any bad news can be that bad".

"Perhaps and perhaps not, Mr. Chowkins, nevertheless, I think you should hear me out". "Do you intend to inform your newspaper about what you experienced in the laboratory, Mr. Chowkins?"

"After what you put me through, I don't see why I shouldn't"

"I can assure you Mr. Chowkins that you will never do that. Understand quite well that any report on this incident will never see the light of day".

Jeremy Chowkins slowly placed his tea-cup and saucer down on the table and for a few seconds stared at Barnistry before he said, "Are you threatening me, Professor Barnistry?"

"Oh no, not in the slightest. You are free to walk out of here and report what you experienced to anyone you like or to any newspaper you like. The only problem is you will be a laughing stock if you do so and furthermore I can't think which newspaper will be interested in your story".

"Well, the newspaper which I work for, *The London Daily*. I am that newspaper's top investigative reporter."

"Mmmm, Mmmmm – *The London Daily* – *The London Daily,* mused Barnistry. Oooo, I eh must say that I've never heard of such a publication."

"It's a new one. It only started up about a week ago."

"I assure you, Mr. Chowkins, that there never was such a newspaper, there isn't, and there never will be".

"Oh, what presumption", Chowkins blurted out. "I work for that paper. Mr. Robert Clout is its editor and he is my employer."

Barnistry simply looked at Chowkins pityingly shaking his head. Without saying anything further, he opened his briefcase and took out a piece of paper. He handed Chowkins the paper and invited him to read it.

I, Jeremy Chowkins do hereby completely and totally agree to release my former wife, Mrs. Samantha Chowkins (who has now reverted to her maiden name 'Giltsilver',) from all oaths and obligations contracted during the marriage ceremony which brought her and I together in wedlock.

I, the same Jeremy Chowkins, do hereby declare that I shall transfer into the name of Ms. Samantha Giltsilver (formerly Mrs. Samantha Chowkins) the house which is currently in my name and which is located in Queen Anne Street, London and whose number is 24. This transfer shall include all items,

> *both moveable and immovable, which are currently contained within the aforesaid property.*
>
> *Finally, I, the above-mentioned and below-signed Jeremy Chowkins, agree to transfer into the name of the above-mentioned Ms. Giltsilver (formerly Chowkins) all assets currently in my name — stock and shareholdings, bank accounts, and physical and material goods.*

Chowkins, absolutely livid, rose from his seat. "Professor Barnistry, what is this fraudulent document, this piece of utter garbage, you have just thrust into my hand. I have never agreed to any such things nor have I seen this document before now let alone appended my signature to it."

"Oh but my dear Mr. Chowkins, you have appended your signature to it. If you would just calm yourself down for a few seconds and look at the bottom of the document".

Chowkins did so and saw his usual signature at the bottom of the document.

"You, you, tricked me into this", said Chowkins furiously.

"That is the document which you willingly signed earlier today in the laboratory".

"I agreed to sign a piece of paper in order to satisfy Samantha of my true identity and whereabouts."

"That is only your word, Mr. Chowkins. You cannot prove it. Such a contention would never hold up in a court of law should you fail to implement the terms of the contract which you have signed".

"Professor Barnistry, you are interfering in my personal and private life. That Samantha works in your company is immaterial; her personal life, like mine, is of no concern to you. Keep your snout out, Professor, mind your own business!" hollered Chowkins.

"Well, you see, Mr. Chowkins, it is my business. Samantha is my niece. I am her maternal uncle."

Chowkins' jaw dropped. He stood there agape. His fury rapidly gave way to total devastation.

"I, I, need a cigarette to steady my nerves", stammered Chowkins.

"Oh, I didn't know you were a smoker", said the professor in surprise.

"Well, I am now", whimpered Chowkins.

"I'm not a smoker myself, but I'll see what I can do for you". With that Barnistry left the office. Five minutes later he returned with a packet of cigarettes and a cigarette lighter. He proceeded to hand these items to Jeremy Chowkins.

"You are right, Professor. I am not a smoker and have no intention of becoming one. Now observe, professor."

Chowkins took the document he had just read and held it by the top right hand corner. Then, he took the cigarette lighter, flicked it and applied its flame to the bottom of the document. With a look of gleeful satisfaction, he watched the document burn to ash. Barnistry watched this performance with total calmness.

"A most entertaining show, Mr. Chowkins, but I'm afraid you're going to have to do better than that. The fact is that you signed multiple copies of the same document. Now you don't think, do you, that I'd be so dumb as to put the sole document in your hands and then hand you a cigarette lighter?"

"And where are these other copies, Professor?"

"There's one here", said a familiar voice from outside the office. In walked Samantha Giltsilver.

"Samantha, in the name of obedience, according to the rules of our game, you destroy that document this instant. I command you".

Samantha and the professor burst into fits of laughter. More laughter was heard as Mr. Lawrence Giltsilver, his wife Mrs. Ruby Giltsilver and Mr. Robert Clout entered the office carrying other duplicates of the document.

"Mr. Clout, sir, you'll back me up in all of this. This professor here has been up to some rather dubious experiments. Now if all this came out in the press...."

"I am not Robert Clout. My name is Barnaby Giltsilver and a partner in *Giltsilver Trading*."

"B bbbb but wh wh what about the newspaper – *The London Daily?*"

"It doesn't exist. There is no such publication".

"I told you that your story would never see the light of day", said Professor Barnistry.

"There are other newspapers", snapped Chowkins. "And there are these patients who were deprived of their bodies and simply left as disembodied heads. They'll testify to the dubious goings-on at this place".

At this point, Peter Porter walked in laughing hilariously. He also was carrying a copy of the document.

"Ha haaa haaa. That was all a trick using dim lights, shadows and sophisticated holographic equipment."

"That's a downright lie. I not only saw it for myself, I even experienced it".

Everyone burst into the most raucous laughter. Barnistry almost fell off the chair and Lawrence Giltsilver almost choked himself to death!

"Come, come, said Peter Porter. If you don't believe me, I'll show you exactly how it was done."

When Peter Porter and Chowkins returned to the office, the laughter had died down but the air of merriment and amusement was still in the air.

"I'm still not convinced", said Chowkins. I had no body when I was in there."

"Because", explained the professor, "I applied to you a new form of anesthetic which I have developed here. It anesthetises all your anatomy except your head."

"Why should I believe that?" said Chowkins somewhat sceptically.

"Look at this video I made of you just after you were given the knock out drug."

"The video footage clearly showed Chowkins being grabbed from behind and then drugged. The anesthetic was applied and Chowkins was taken to one of the pillar type structures. The back of the pillar was open and Chowkins' trunk could be seen. He was strapped to a chair with his arms outstretched and tied to a support within the pillar."

"Now see", said Barnistry, "here is a rear view of you signing the document with your de-anesthetised hand."

"And all that about the thousands of miniature organs under the head, being grown from DNA and changed every day?"

Everyone again descended into fits of uncontrollable laughter. Chowkins looked around himself feeling completely stupid.

"The only organ I can use to describe all that, Mr. Chowkins", laughed the professor, "is this – bollocks".

"You're a Philosophy major aren't you Jeremy?" said Ruby Giltsilver. "It's just a pity that you didn't use it."

"You see Jeremy", said Lawrence Giltsilver, "you thought you were being so clever, so witty, but in the end you simply turned out to be the fox who out-foxed himself".

XIII.

In a rich neighbourhood in London, two men are digging up the street. They have been digging for the past two hours and decide that it is time for their tea-break. They get the brazier burning and start the brewing up process.

"I still keeps tryin the lo'ery an' an football pools. Yi never know, I mights just strike it lucky one of 'em days. It would be great ti be rich an' live in one of 'em 'ouses like them toffs do, yi know. I wouldn't 'ave to buva diggin' up any more o' 'em streets."

The labourer then got up from his rickety old wooden bench. And in the middle of the street, and still holding his tin cup of tea, he started singing and dancing. The traffic was held up, passers-by gawked in amazement and windows were flung open by the street's residents who wanted to find out what all the commotion was about. The street digger was undeterred:

Dear God, you mades many, many poor people.
I realise, of course, that it's no shame to be poor.
But it's no great honor either!
So, wot would 'ave been so terrible hif I 'ad a small fortune?"

Sadly there were no talent spotters around – or – maybe there were. But after this strange performance, the man with the First Class Honours Degree in Philosophy from no less a seat of learning that the University of Brixton, laid down his tin cup, took up his pick ax and started digging. There was no-one nearby who appeared to be interested in a cockneyised version of the song from Fiddler on the Roof. The street digger was perfectly resigned to his fate and did nothing to challenge those who had been responsible for it incase it was ever discovered who exactly was the fiddler in the board-room.